### *"I want a mommy,"*

Lucy whispered in Sherrie's ear.

Sherrie had to clear her throat. "Well, Lucy, that's quite a wish. I'll tell Santa what you want, but you do understand he can't always bring children what they ask for."

Lucy listened gravely to the practiced speech, her eyes fixed on Mrs. Claus's face. She sighed. "I just want a mommy. Daddy and me are very lonely."

Sherrie looked into those liquid blue eyes and felt her heart melt. Scrooge himself couldn't have denied the appeal in that face. "Well, sweetheart," she said softly, "we'll just have to see what we can do, won't we?"

Dear Reader,

What better way for Silhouette Romance to celebrate the holiday season than to celebrate the meaning of family....

You'll love the way a confirmed bachelor becomes a FABULOUS FATHER just in time for the holidays in Susan Meier's *Merry Christmas, Daddy*. And in *Mistletoe Bride*, Linda Varner's HOME FOR THE HOLIDAYS miniseries merrily continues. The ugly duckling who becomes a beautiful swan will touch your heart in *Hometown Wedding* by Elizabeth Lane. Doreen Roberts's *A Mom for Christmas* tells the tale of a little girl's holiday wish, and in Patti Standard's *Family of the Year*, one man, one woman and a bunch of adorable kids form an unexpected family. And finally, *Christmas in July* by Leanna Wilson is what a sexy cowboy offers the struggling single mom he wants for his own.

Silhouette Romance novels make the perfect stocking stuffers—or special treats just for yourself. So enjoy all six irresistible books, and most of all, have a very happy holiday season and a very happy New Year!

Melissa Senate
Senior Editor
Silhouette Romance

Please address questions and book requests to:
Silhouette Reader Service
U.S.: 3010 Walden Ave., P.O. Box 1325, Buffalo, NY 14269
Canadian: P.O. Box 609, Fort Erie, Ont. L2A 5X3

# A MOM FOR CHRISTMAS

## Doreen Roberts

Silhouette

R O M A N C E™

Published by Silhouette Books

America's Publisher of Contemporary Romance

To Bill, who makes every day of the year
as special as Christmas.

SILHOUETTE BOOKS

ISBN 0-373-19195-2

A MOM FOR CHRISTMAS

Copyright © 1996 by Doreen Roberts

**Printed in U.S.A.**

## DOREEN ROBERTS

has an ambition to visit every state in the United States. She recently added several to her list when she drove across the country to spend a year on the East Coast. She's thinking about setting her future books in each of the states she has visited. She has now returned to settle down in Oregon with her new husband, and to get back to doing what she loves most—writing books about adventurous people who just happen to fall in love.

# What I Want for Christmas
## By
## Lucy Blanchard

1. A mommy
2. A mommy
3. A mommy
4. A wife for Daddy

xoxo

# Chapter One

Christmas, Matthew Blanchard kept reminding himself, was traditionally the season to be jolly. He was doing his level best to live up to that optimistic theory. He might have done a better job of it had he not been staring at a total disaster smack-dab in the middle of his Christmas display.

Every year, on the Monday after Thanksgiving, the fifth floor of Blanchard's Department Store was transformed into a children's fantasyland. And Matt had gone all out on this year's Santa Claus display.

Life-size animated reindeer stood on either side of the dais, their curly eyelashes blinking and their majestic antlers solemnly swaying back and forth as each child came forward to greet Santa.

A spectacular Christmas tree stood at the back of the platform, its thick branches loaded down with red and white ornaments, twinkling lights and packages wrapped with bright ribbon bows. Close by, cardboard elves peeked from the windows of a six-foot-high gingerbread house, which was smothered in candy canes and jelly beans, while a lifelike Mrs. Claus smiled from the peppermint-studded doorway.

In the middle of all this glittering splendor sat a huge red velvet chair, and it was there that Matt's gaze was focused in sheer disbelief. The plump, jolly old gentleman—mankind's fond image of Santa Claus—was noticeably absent. In his place sat a ridiculous miniature of that esteemed character.

It seemed to Matt as if the damn chair swallowed up the red-suited figure. The fur-lined cap rested precariously on Santa's lopsided eyebrows, and his feet swung an inch or two off the floor. As an added highlight, instead of boots, the delicate feet sported a pair of elegant, black high-heeled shoes.

Matt waited with barely controlled patience until the tousle-haired boy with freckles had scrambled down from Santa's ridiculously small lap. Then, drawing in a deep, slow breath, he marched up to the dais, mounted it and held up an imperious hand.

"I'm sorry, children," he announced, baring his teeth in the best semblance of a smile he could muster, "but I'm afraid it's time for Santa's break. He'll be back soon, I promise you."

His voice had cracked on the *he,* which did not improve his temper. Neither did the shouts of dismay from the waiting children and their weary mothers. With a curt beckoning motion for Santa to follow, Matt stormed across the crowded floor, heading for his office.

Matthew Blanchard did not tolerate mistakes easily. He particularly did not like someone else messing up his carefully executed preparations. Someone had made a big mistake this time, and heads were going to roll.

If it had been any other time but Christmas, he might have held on to his temper. But then, if it had been any other time but Christmas, there wouldn't have been a miniature Santa in high heels to bother him. And he wouldn't have had to worry about disappointing Lucy.

Normally Matt could handle the ups and downs of being a single father. There were even times when he managed to convince himself that things were better that way, and that he had a more satisfying relationship with his five-year-old daughter without a mother to divide Lucy's attention. Until Christmas.

Christmas, somehow, was different. Christmas was the time for families, whole families, kids with both parents, and especially a mother to bake cookies and wrap gifts and write Christmas cards and go shopping with...especially the shopping.

Yes, Christmas was definitely a bad time of year for a single father. Matt looked forward to the entire season with a kind of gnawing anxiety that grew worse as Christmas Day drew closer. He was therefore in no mood to deal with the kind of debacle he'd just witnessed.

He reached the door of his office, doing his best to cool his temper. He had to wait quite some time for Santa to catch up with him, which wasn't terribly surprising. The pants of the bright red costume were crumpled above the dainty shoes like elephant skin. They dragged on the floor behind, severely hampering the figure inside.

Finally Santa stood silently in front of his desk. And what a sorry picture he made, Matt thought in disgust. The white fur hem of the red coat reached almost to the ankles, and the sleeves dangled dismally, completely obliterating any sign of hands.

Matt glared at the sea green eyes peeking out at him from behind the cloud of white cotton-ball hair and fuzzy beard. The wary expression in those eyes satisfied Matt. Santa had every reason to be wary. Matt could feel his temper gathering momentum like storm clouds across an angry sea.

He raked his gaze up and down the short, bulging figure, which, judging by the lumps and bumps, had been created by a lousy job of padding. "I seem to remember," he said carefully, "that when I hired you, you were around five feet ten, weighing somewhere around two hundred pounds, with a voice that sounded like a marine sergeant."

The voice that answered him was nothing like a marine sergeant's. It reminded him more of a mermaid, for some reason, though he couldn't imagine for the life of him what a mermaid would actually sound like.

"That was my brother, Tom Latimer, Mr. Blanchard. I'm Sherrie Latimer."

"Really." He struggled with his temper for a moment before continuing in a voice heavily laced with sarcasm. "Then perhaps you will be so kind as to tell me where your brother might be? In the hospital, I presume? I will accept no other excuse for this ridiculous charade."

"Er... Tom is in Mexico, Mr. Blanchard. He told me he'd informed you of the new arrangements."

"Mexico," Matt echoed, through gritted teeth. "How nice for him. And no, he did not inform me of his plans. Had he done so, I would have ordered him in here on the double, threatening to sue the pants off him for breach of contract if he didn't make it."

"I'm sorry, Mr. Blanchard, but—"

"Sorry? I'm the one who's sorry, Miss Latimer. As no doubt you are aware, I happen to own the biggest department store in Westmill, Oregon. Hundreds of children look forward every year to visiting Santa, bringing their parents with them to shop in my store. I spend a great deal of money making sure they are not disappointed."

He knew his voice was rising, but he couldn't seem to control it. Before Santa had time to say anything he continued at a near roar. "My Christmas display gets more ambitious and more damn expensive every year. But it's something the children, and their parents, have come to expect from a prestigious store like Blanchard's."

Warming up now, he paused for breath. Sherrie Latimer opened her mouth, but he forestalled her. "Therefore, I am entitled to feel a tad put out if the centerpiece of this ambitious and, I might add, outrageously expensive display, the focal point of this spectacular display... the jolly old gentleman of Christmas himself... turns out to be a sawed-off substitute in high heels!"

"Excuse me?" The substitute Santa's voice had garnered considerable strength.

Matt watched, fascinated in spite of himself, as a small, delicate hand wriggled out from the bottom of a sleeve and swept up to Santa's head. Grabbing the hat, the hand tugged it off, taking with it most of the white hair.

A mass of amber curls spilled onto the padded shoulders of the suit. The hand let go of the hat, and tugged at the mustache and beard. A sharp "Ouch!" accompanied the gesture. Then the voice spoke again, as clear and as cool as a Christmas bell.

"You have absolutely no excuse for speaking to me in that disgraceful tone of voice. I am not some disobedient child you can intimidate with your insults. I am a grown woman, and as such, I demand a certain amount of respect."

Matt peered at the flushed face in front of him. Wisps of white cotton clung to the curls at the forehead and over one ear. The mustache had left a thin wisp of white above the most attractive mouth he'd ever seen, and still more clung to the determined, slightly pointed chin. In spite of his temper, Matt felt an insane urge to smile.

He might have smiled, if he hadn't been shocked to realize that this was no inept teenager, as he'd first imagined, standing in front of him with that rebellious scowl on her face. "How old are you?" he demanded, without thinking.

"That, Mr. Blanchard, is an impertinent and totally irrelevant question. It's enough for you to know that I am old enough to be spoken to in a civil manner."

Aware that she was right, he resorted to his gruffest tone. "My apologies, Miss Latimer. And since you are, as you say, a responsible adult, perhaps you will enlighten me as to why your brother felt it perfectly all right to run off to Mexico for a last-minute vacation and leave a... woman... to play the part of Santa Claus."

Behind the wisps of cotton he saw two delicate eyebrows arch. "You have something against women, Mr. Blanchard? I do believe that comes under the category of discrimination."

Matt buried his face in his hands, raking his hair with his fingers. "Oh, give me a break." He slowly let out his breath, then added heavily, "No, I do not have anything against women. What I do have a thing against is a Santa Claus who..." He paused once more, searching for a more diplomatic way to say what was on the tip of his tongue.

The toe of one shoe lifted up and down on the thick carpet. He caught the movement out of the corner of his eye, and gritted his teeth. "Miss Latimer. I ask you to be honest when you answer this question. Describe to me your idea of Santa Claus as if you were a child who still believed in him."

She was silent for so long he wondered if she was refusing to answer. Then, in a slightly less belligerent voice, she said, "I admit, I'm not as tall as most Santas, but I am sitting down almost all of the time. With the padding and the beard, the children can't really tell the difference."

"Until you open your mouth," Matt said darkly.

"I lower my voice."

She had spoken the words an octave deeper, which merely made her sound as if she had a bad cold. There was no way in hell that voice could be mistaken for a man's.

"The point, Miss Latimer," Matt said, as patiently as he could manage considering he was still steaming, "is that I hired your brother for the job. I go to a great deal of trouble to pick the right person to play the part of Santa. Not only does he have to look the part and sound the part, he has to act the part as well. If I might say so, Miss Latimer, you don't look much bigger than a child yourself."

"I happen to be five feet five in my heels."

"Which is another thing." Matt pressed his point home. "In my entire life, which amounts to a little less than forty years, I have never, ever, seen a Santa wearing high-heeled shoes."

"They make me look taller."

"They make Santa Claus look ridiculous, if you'll forgive me for saying so."

"You're entitled to your opinion."

He could almost see the frost on her breath. And the hot sparkle in those remarkable green eyes was really something to watch. With a start he pulled himself together. "You didn't answer my question," he said abruptly.

"Which question was that, Mr. Blanchard?"

Her constant use of his last name was beginning to get on his nerves, for some reason. She made it sound as if he had one foot in the grave. She couldn't be that much younger than he, for pity's sake.

He cleared his throat, loudly, as if to silence the inner voice. "I would like to know why your brother made these last-minute arrangements and why I wasn't informed in time to hire someone else."

"My brother," Miss Latimer said coldly, "is with a mercy mission team traveling to Mexico to bring some small vision of Christmas cheer to underprivileged, underfed children who have little conception of what Christmas is all about. They have never owned expensive toys, let alone played with them. And they have never seen expensive, commercialized displays in overpriced toy departments. Neither have they ever spoken to a fake Santa Claus and judged whether he looked real or not."

Taken aback, Matt allowed several seconds to go by while he recovered his voice. "Your brother's mission is very commendable, I'm sure. That does not, however, excuse him from deliberately ignoring his contract with me. Or explain why he entered into it in the first place if he intended to spend Christmas in Mexico."

"He didn't know he was going to Mexico until yesterday afternoon. Somebody had to drop out at the last minute and the organization people were desperately hunting for a substitute. If you knew my brother, Mr. Blanchard, you would understand. This is a project very close to his heart. He couldn't turn them down."

"Certainly not as easily as he could turn me down, apparently," Matt said, struggling to hold on to his resentment. There was something about this young woman that threatened to make him forget why he was angry with her.

"He tried everywhere to get someone else to take the Santa job. He's been playing Santa for years at different stores in Portland. When you're in construction you have plenty of time off in the winter, and he loves the job."

"Yes, he told me. That's why I hired him." Matt leaned back in his chair and let his gaze travel over her suit's bulging padding again. "And because he looked the part."

"I'm sorry, Mr. Blanchard," Sherrie Latimer said, sounding not a bit apologetic at all, "but I was the only one available. I agreed to do it for him."

"Under protest, by all accounts," Matt said dryly, remembering the caustic comments about commercialized, overpriced displays. "You must love your brother a great deal."

"I do. He's the only one I've got."

Matt felt a moment of envy for Tom Latimer, then quickly squashed the thought. "The fact remains, you do not bear the slightest resemblance to your brother in any shape or form, and no matter how high the heels of your shoes, or how deep you pitch your voice, there is not one child within a hundred miles of here who is going to believe for an instant that *you* are Santa Claus. In fact, if I allow you to continue this farce, Blanchard's will be the laughingstock of the town."

"We can't let the children down, Mr. Blanchard. Most of them know that Santa can't be everywhere, anyway. They look upon us more as Santa's helpers."

"I know, I know. Even so, you just don't look the part. Not by any stretch of the imagination." He reached for a pencil and tapped it irritably on the table. "Well, I guess there isn't much I can do about it today. You can finish the day out, while I try to find a replacement. Though heaven knows where I'm going to find one at this late date."

"I do have a suggestion," Sherrie Latimer said, a little hesitantly.

He'd heard just about enough explanations from her. Nevertheless, he was near desperation himself. How Lucy was going to take this he had no idea. That thought irritated him more than anything. He might not be able to provide a proper family Christmas without a mother, but he could at least make his daughter's visit with Santa Claus a very special treat. At least, he could have managed until today.

"Go ahead," he said, resting his fingers against his eyes. "It can't be any worse than what we've got."

"I could be Mrs. Santa Claus. The clothes the mannequin is wearing in the gingerbread house should fit me much better, and we could dress up a mannequin as Santa and have him in the doorway of the house. I'll just tell the children that the real Santa is busy with the elves at the North Pole and he sent his wife instead."

Very slowly, Matt lowered his hand. Brilliant. Absolutely brilliant. He would be the only store to have a Mrs. Claus, which would surely gain points with the mothers. The whole concept could bring even more curious people into his store, just to get a look. He might even swing a spot on local television and get some free publicity.

He looked steadily at Sherrie Latimer for a long moment, noticing with a small sense of satisfaction that she seemed to fidget under his gaze. "That might work," he said, letting just the right amount of doubt creep into his voice.

It wouldn't do to let her know how pleased he was with the idea. In his experience, if he offered someone as young as Miss Latimer an apple she was likely to turn it into an entire orchard. No, let her think he was grudgingly allowing her to try to make up for her brother's mistake. She would be far more likely to work her butt off proving she was right.

He just hoped she had the stamina for the job. Playing Santa was a grueling experience, judging from the comments of his past employees. "Are you sure you can handle it?" he asked, letting his gaze flick over her padded figure. "It's a tough job for a woman."

As he'd hoped, her chin came up a fraction. "If my brother can handle it, then so can I. Tom would feel very badly if the children were deprived of a Santa. I really do think Mrs. Claus would be a hundred times better than no Santa at all."

"Yes, well, that remains to be seen. I guess it couldn't hurt for now, anyway." He reached for the phone and dialed the warehouse. "Yes, take a male mannequin to toys as quickly as possible. I need the clothes on the mannequin in the Santa display in my office. Do it as discreetly as possible, and have someone let the customers know that Santa will be there soon."

He replaced the receiver and looked back at Sherrie Latimer who was staring at the picture of Lucy on his desk. He waited for a comment, but she hastily directed her gaze back to his face.

After a moment of awkward silence, he asked heavily, "When you aren't bailing your brother out of trouble, Miss Latimer, what do you do for a living?"

"I'm a research assistant for Conway Pharmaceuticals." She touched her lips with her fingers and dislodged some more cotton.

He was suitably impressed, but did his darnedest not to show it. "You must have a very understanding boss to allow you to take off at a minute's notice." Probably more understanding than he was at the moment, he grudgingly admitted.

To his surprise, Sherrie Latimer didn't answer right away. In fact, she appeared to be having some trouble with her eyes, since they were tightly shut. Just when he was on the point of asking her if she was all right, she opened her eyes and blinked several times.

"I happen to be on vacation, Mr. Blanchard. I had intended to spend the holidays with my brother, until this emergency came up."

He could swear he saw a tear glistening in her eye. No doubt she was terribly disappointed that her plans for Christmas had been upset. He was beginning to feel like a prize jerk for yelling at her and was relieved when a sharp tap on the door interrupted the conversation.

As he took Mrs. Claus's clothes from the arms of the young man at the door, a thought flashed through his mind. He wondered what kind of figure Sherrie Latimer was hiding under all that padding.

Annoyed with himself, he practically threw the outfit into her arms. "I'll get out of here while you change," he muttered. "Lock the door behind me and when you're finished, take the Santa suit down to toys and have someone dress the mannequin and put it back in the house."

"Yes, Mr. Blanchard."

The words had been polite enough, but he'd detected a note of rebellion in the quiet voice.

"Please," he added, as an afterthought, then wondered what the hell was the matter with him. He was her boss, after all. Even if it was temporary.

Deciding the best thing he could do was to get out of there as quickly as possible, he gave her a brief nod and escaped through the door. The firm click of the lock behind him seemed to echo in his mind as he strode down the hallway.

Inside the office Sherrie scrambled out of the Santa suit, breathing a sigh of relief. Tom would have been upset if she'd messed things up for him. He'd been so torn between the chance to go to Mexico and his responsibility to Blanchard's, not to mention letting down the hordes of children eagerly waiting to meet Santa. Most of all, he'd been worried about leaving her on her own for the holidays.

In fact, it had taken a superb acting job on her part to convince him she'd be perfectly happy by herself. She had nowhere else to go, she'd pointed out, and she certainly didn't feel like facing her friends after the fiasco at the church.

Sherrie stepped out of the roomy pants, struggling with the sudden onslaught of depression. It was bad enough that she'd been jilted practically at the altar, leaving her a month's vacation to get through.

Instead of spending two weeks in Hawaii on her honeymoon and another two moving into a new, expensive condo, she was now faced with the prospect of finding somewhere cheaper to live, since she'd already moved out of her old apartment.

With her furniture in storage, and unable to bear the thought of everyone feeling sorry for her, Sherrie had immediately agreed when Tom had suggested she stay with him until she found somewhere else to go.

It had seemed the perfect solution. Tom wasn't the kind to commiserate with her. He'd told her flat out that Jason's last-minute cold feet was the best thing that could have happened to her. Knowing that he was right was poor consolation, however. Spending the holidays alone in her brother's apartment was not her idea of celebrating Christmas, and playing Santa for a crowd of excitable, hyperactive children had definitely not entered into her plans.

Nevertheless, once she made a commitment, she stuck with it. Through heaven and hell, if need be. She'd promised Tom she would do the job for him, and Sherrie Latimer always kept a promise. Even if Matthew Blanchard did not approve of her. Besides, playing Santa would at least keep her mind off her own troubles.

Sherrie eyed the Mrs. Claus outfit with a frown. It was still too big for her, but a vast improvement on the suffocating red wool suit that now lay crumpled on the floor amid a pile of pillows.

The full skirted dress with the red-and-green holly pattern slipped easily over her head. She added a pillow to give her a bosom, and another under the waistband, then pulled on the white wig and the bonnet.

Placing the pair of granny glasses on the edge of her nose, she squinted through the empty frames. She wished she had a full-length mirror to inspect herself before she went public. Matthew Blanchard didn't have one mirror in the entire room. Obviously he didn't like looking at himself.

Which was too bad, Sherrie thought, as she bent over to pick up the Santa suit. The man would be quite attractive if he learned to smile.

The glasses slid down her nose and fell to the floor. She reached for them, grunting as the pillows prevented her from bending that far. She almost toppled over as she made a grab for the spectacles.

Straightening again, she let out a long sigh. She was clumsy enough as it was, without having to deal with the unfamiliar padding obstructing her every movement. Heaven help her if she dropped a child off her lap.

After folding the red coat neatly, she laid it on the uncluttered desk. The photo of the little girl was turned partly away from her, and Sherrie couldn't resist taking a closer look. Turning the frame toward her, she saw a pretty child of about four or five.

It was obvious the little girl was Matthew Blanchard's daughter. She had the same gaunt cheekbones, straight nose and light blue eyes, though her hair was dark blond instead of black like her father's. Her smile lit up her entire face, in stark contrast to her father's grim, austere expression, but even so, she bore a marked resemblance to Sherrie's temporary boss.

Sherrie turned the frame back to its original position, wondering what the little girl's mother looked like, and why her picture wasn't on Matthew Blanchard's desk beside his daughter's. Deciding it was none of her business, she folded up the rest of Santa's suit, then bundled it under her arm. It was time to get back to work.

An hour or so later, Sherrie was beginning to wish she had never agreed to take Tom's place. Why her brother enjoyed the job, she couldn't imagine. His instructions had seemed simple enough—greet the children, ask them if they'd been good, ask them what they wanted for Christmas, never promise to deliver but tell them she'd see what she could do, throw in a couple of *Ho Ho Ho*s, give them a candy cane and go on to the next one.

What he hadn't told her was that children could be remarkably curious and sometimes downright personal. One little girl had asked her if she and Santa slept in the same bed, and one smart-mouthed boy, who couldn't have been more than ten, asked her for a date.

Another little girl, who had sat in silence for so long Sherrie had just about given up on getting a word out of her, suddenly asked in a loud voice what kind of underwear Mrs. Claus wore at the North Pole.

Question after question poured from their eager lips. What was it like to be married to Santa? Did she get lonely when he was out delivering the toys? What kind of dinners did she cook for him?

When she did finally manage to get in a couple of questions of her own, some children boldly demanded everything from sports cars and motorbikes to automatic rifles.

More than one handed her a list as long as a toilet roll, while others touched her heart by asking for nothing more than a new sweater or a jacket. Those were the ones she wished she could take into the clothing department and let them pick out whatever they wanted.

After delivering a screaming child back to its determined parent, Sherrie longed for a break. Her back ached from the constant hauling up and down of dozens of kids, some of whom weighed almost as much as she did.

A glance at her watch told her she had about ten minutes to go when she caught sight of Blanchard's owner heading through the crowds around the toy department. He was almost up to her before she saw the small child he led by the hand.

She was a fragile little girl, with dark blond curls embracing an unsmiling, heart-shaped face. She looked up with a wistful expression when the tall man at her side spoke to her.

Sherrie braced herself. If her memory served her right, she was about to meet Matthew Blanchard's daughter.

She was quite impressed when the store owner stood patiently in line, holding his daughter's hand. Saying goodbye to her break for a while longer, Sherrie concentrated on the children ahead of her boss.

At last it was the solemn little girl's turn. Matthew Blanchard stood discreetly back from the platform as the child sat stiffly on the edge of Sherrie's knees. The little girl seemed to weigh hardly anything at all, and her blue eyes were huge in her delicate face.

"Can you tell me your name?" Sherrie asked, and was rewarded with a soft whisper.

"Lucy Blanchard."

"Lucy. That's a nice name." Sherrie smiled, forgetting for the moment that the child's formidable father stood just a few feet away. "I can tell you've been a good girl. What would you like me to ask Santa to bring you for Christmas?"

Lucy stared at her, as if she wasn't sure she understood the question. "Daddy said Santa couldn't come."

Sherrie nodded. "I'm afraid Santa is really busy getting all the toys ready for Christmas Eve. But I'll be talking to him before he leaves the North Pole on his sleigh, so you can tell me what you want. I'll make sure he gets the message, okay?"

"Okay."

Sherrie waited a moment, while the little girl continued to study her face. "Is there something you really want for Christmas?" she prompted, when Lucy seemed content to remain silent.

Lucy nodded, then looked over her shoulder at her father, who was watching the kids in the toy department trying out everything on the shelves. Apparently reassured, the little girl leaned forward to put her mouth close to Sherrie's ear.

"I want a mommy," she whispered.

Her hair tickled Sherrie's ear, and she wasn't sure she'd heard right. "You mean a mommy doll?"

Lucy shook her head. "A real mommy."

Sherrie felt cold, as if someone had turned on the air-conditioning. "You don't have a mommy?"

Again Lucy shook her head, her beautiful eyes pleading with Sherrie to understand.

Sherrie had to clear her throat. "Well, Lucy, that's quite a wish. I'll be sure to tell Santa what you want, but you do understand he can't always bring children what they ask for. He will do his very best, and I'm sure you'll be happy with whatever he does bring for you."

Lucy listened gravely to the practiced speech, her eyes fixed on Mrs. Claus's face. She seemed to think about it for a while, then she let out a small sigh. "I just want a mommy. Daddy and me is very lonely."

Sherrie looked into those liquid blue eyes and felt her heart melt. Scrooge himself couldn't have denied the appeal in that face. "Well, sweetheart," she said softly, "we'll just have to see what we can do, won't we?"

# Chapter Two

Later, in Tom's apartment, Sherrie sank onto the shabby couch with a weary sigh. By the time she finished playing Mrs. Claus next month, she thought ruefully, she'd have muscles Mr. Universe would envy. Thank heavens the job was only four hours a day. Any longer than that and someone would have to carry her out of the place.

After the noisy chatter of the children, she welcomed the quiet peace of the silent room. Leaning her back against a soft, plump pillow, she closed her eyes and tried to empty her mind.

Gradually the clamor of excited voices began to fade until all that was left was the wistful whisper of a sad-faced little girl.

Sherrie opened her eyes again and sat up. Now that she had time to think about it, she was beginning to realize just what she had taken on. She had more or less promised a trusting child that she would find her a mother.

Even more daunting was the other side to that particular coin. She would have to find a wife for Matthew Blanchard.

No longer feeling relaxed, Sherrie jumped up and went into Tom's tiny kitchen. She had set herself a formidable task, she thought, as she studied the meager contents of the ancient fridge. She would have to find a very special woman, someone with a heart full of love to give to a lonely little girl.

That would be difficult enough. Finding someone who was willing to take on Matthew Blanchard as part of the deal might be darn well impossible.

She would give a great deal to know what had happened to Lucy's mother. It could have been a divorce, or perhaps the mother had died. Either way, Lucy must miss her mother a great deal. She would be hard to replace.

Sherrie closed the door of the fridge with a shudder and opened up a cabinet. The only item that looked remotely appetizing was a packet of macaroni and cheese. Obviously her brother was not fond of eating at home.

Sighing, she reached for the packet and made a mental note to shop on the way home from the store the next day.

After dinner, Sherrie tried to concentrate on a television program, but the vision of Lucy Blanchard's pensive face kept getting in the way. To make matters worse, the stern features of Lucy's father also kept intruding on her thoughts.

Finally giving up, Sherrie switched off the television and thought of the task she'd set for herself. Lucy would present no problem, once Mrs. Claus had found the right woman. It was Matthew Blanchard who presented the biggest obstacle.

Impatient with herself, Sherrie went back into the kitchen to make a cup of hot chocolate. She didn't know enough about the man to make a fair judgment, she told herself. First impressions could be misleading and, after all, he had a lot going in his favor.

In the first place, he was nice-looking. Attractive, even, if one went for the strong, intense type. He was obviously well-off, since he owned the largest department store in town. If only he would lighten up and smile now and again, he'd be quite a catch—as long as someone was willing to make the effort to break through that intimidating front he presented.

All she had to do, Sherrie decided as she crawled into bed, was find the right woman. Out of all the single women she knew, there had to be someone who would be perfect for Lucy and her implacable father.

Having convinced herself on that score, Sherrie did her best to go to sleep. It wasn't easy. Alone in the unfamiliar apartment, every sound seemed ominous. Tom had intended to sleep on the couch while she was staying with him, and she couldn't help wishing he hadn't had to leave.

Now that she had nothing to do but think, Jason's last-minute betrayal seemed catastrophic. She had lost much more than a future husband. She'd given up her cozy home in a familiar neighborhood where she knew most of the locals. But even if her apartment hadn't been rented, she knew she wouldn't return there.

She preferred to make a completely new start in a place where no one knew she'd been dumped at the altar. As for Jason, he had completely destroyed her trust in men. In her opinion, marriage was overrated and risky at best. She could only hope that Matthew Blanchard's new wife would have better luck.

Annoyed with the way her mind kept returning to her unapproachable boss, she turned on her side and tried to get comfortable. Tom's apartment could use some new furniture, she thought, as she pummeled the pillow. It could also use a woman's touch—something pretty on the walls would help cheer up the place. Her brother really needed a wife as well.

She smiled to herself in the darkness. If she could find a wife for Matthew Blanchard, finding one for Tom would be a breeze. On that happy thought, she drifted off to sleep.

Matt just happened to be standing near the employees' entrance when Sherrie Latimer arrived the next morning. He'd convinced himself that he was merely checking to make sure she was going to turn up for work. After all, she'd looked pretty tired by the end of her shift yesterday.

He refused to even consider the possibility that he wanted to see her arrive for the sole purpose of checking out her figure. Not even when his pulse leapt as she came through the door.

He'd forgotten the way her honey gold hair with its hint of red curled onto her shoulders. Without the glasses and white wig she looked incredibly young.

She wore a black skirt that barely skimmed her knees, and a black sweater with a yellow-and-black scarf tucked in the neck. Her curvy figure easily surpassed his wildest imagination. He was used to seeing reed-thin athletic bodies on the women at the health club. He hadn't realized how much more exciting it was to look at someone a little more filled out.

His curiosity satisfied, he tried to slip away unnoticed, but she caught sight of him before he could make his escape.

"Good morning, Mr. Blanchard!" she called out, with a slight smile playing around her mouth, as if she knew his heart rate had jumped to jogging level.

He mumbled an answering greeting, then watched her trip lightly over to the elevators. He had to stop this, he thought desperately. She was, after all, one of his employees. He made it a rule never to fraternize with the help.

Not that he wanted to socialize with her, he hastily assured himself as he strode over to the escalator. For one thing, she was too young. For another, he rather suspected that Miss Latimer had very definite ideas on any given subject—ideas that were likely to clash with his own.

She appeared to be the kind of young lady who would have no qualms opposing his views rather strongly if she were so inclined. And if there was one thing Matt hated, it was an argument.

More often than not he gave in, sacrificing his own convictions rather than argue, which had been part of the problem with his ex-wife. If he hadn't been so indulgent with Caroline, if he'd insisted that she behave like a responsible adult instead of condoning her selfish, immature behavior, he might have saved the marriage. Though he rather doubted it.

He was pretty sure that Caroline had never really loved him. Her head had been turned by the big bucks. She'd seen the furs, designer fashions and jewelry that Blanchard's carried and she was like the kids in the toy department. She wanted it all. Until Lucy had come along and put an end to her freedom. Then she hadn't wanted either of them.

Well, he told himself as he rode the crowded escalator to the next floor, he was through with that kind of commitment. Never again. He'd learned a tough lesson. He'd made a mistake and he wasn't about to repeat it. That settled, he resolved to put Miss Latimer and her delectable figure right out of his mind.

Upstairs in the private employees' lounge, Sherrie's bones ached as she dressed in the Mrs. Claus outfit. She adjusted the wig and the glasses and scowled at her image in the mirror. If this was how she would look when she got old, she thought, there wasn't a lot to look forward to.

She was about to leave for her first stint in Santa's chair when the door of the lounge opened. The impeccable, heavily perfumed creature who entered eyed her up and down with amusement.

"God," she muttered, "if I had to spend longer than five minutes in that outfit I'd quit."

"It's not exactly my favorite way to dress," Sherrie said, smiling. "Actually I'm doing it as a favor for my brother. He was supposed to be Santa."

The woman nodded. "So I heard. One of the stockmen told me about the last-minute change. Actually you look pretty good. Definitely an improvement on some of the Santas we've had. How's things going down there?"

"Exhausting," Sherrie admitted. "But I enjoy meeting all the children."

The woman leaned closer to the mirror and patted her immaculate blond hair. Opening the small black purse she carried, she took out a lipstick and touched up her lips.

"My name's Beryl Robbins," she said, slipping the gold case back into her purse. "I'm the head buyer here. We'll probably bump into each other now and again. If you want to know anything about this place, just ask me. There isn't much that gets by me."

Sherrie could well believe that. The woman's sharp brown eyes under the mascara-laden lashes were never still. "I'm Sherrie," she murmured, "and I'll keep it in mind." She slipped out of the door then, before Beryl Robbins could begin probing into her private life.

Down on the fifth floor, the children were already lined up, waiting impatiently for Mrs. Claus to arrive. A small cheer went up as Sherrie took her seat and beckoned to the first little girl in line.

The child's mother held on to the small hand, and seemed determined to do all the talking. It took several moments of diplomatic persuasion before Sherrie could talk to the child herself.

Watching from a discreet distance, Matt felt a small stab of satisfaction. The Mrs. Claus idea seemed to be working out quite well, in spite of the diminutive size of the woman inside the padding. In fact, it amazed him to see her hauling all those kids up onto her lap. He'd expected her to come crying to him at the end of her first day to say she couldn't handle the job.

He felt a little more comfortable now that she was dressed as Mrs. Claus again. It seemed to put a respectable distance between them. After all, who would have the urge to date Santa's wife? Highly inappropriate, to say the least.

After studying the application form he'd had his newest employee fill out, Matt had learned little more about Sherrie Latimer. She was twenty-seven, single and a college graduate. She'd listed her present address as the same as her brother's, which, now that he came to think about it, was a bit odd, since she'd told Matt that she was merely spending the holidays with Tom Latimer.

Remembering the misty-eyed expression he'd noticed when he'd mentioned her holiday plans, Matt wondered if she'd had some kind of trouble. He quickly reminded himself that it was none of his business.

As long as Sherrie Latimer did a good job for him, her private life was her own concern. The position was only temporary anyway. Once the Christmas season was over, he would probably never set eyes on Sherrie Latimer again.

To his dismay, the thought gave him a definite twinge of regret. He turned his back on Mrs. Claus and headed toward the crowded toy department. He wasn't about to let himself get distracted by a ditzy, pint-size angel of mercy who let her heart rule her head.

Any other woman with an atom of sense would have told her brother to find himself another Santa. But obviously she wasn't like other women. She'd given up her vacation and taken on a mammoth task so that her brother could go chasing all over Mexico on his own errand of mercy, as she'd put it.

He would have admired that, if he hadn't been convinced that women like Sherrie Latimer were a danger to self-respecting, confirmed single fathers, who should know better than to spend their mornings wondering if a certain woman tasted as good as she looked.

Seated on her red velvet throne, Sherrie was having her own troubles. One little girl, desperate to go to the bathroom, was determined not to lose her place in line. Unfortunately the wait proved too long, and Sherrie's lap was decidedly damp after the child had scrambled down.

The next small boy demanded that Santa bring him a space gun for Christmas.

"I'll be sure to tell Santa what you would like just as soon as I get back to the North Pole," Sherrie said, reaching for a candy cane.

"I don't want to wait till Christmas," the boy announced, scowling at her, "I want it now."

Sherrie tried to curb her flash of irritation. "Well, I'm afraid you can't have it now. Santa doesn't deliver the toys until Christmas Eve. But you can have a candy cane now."

"Don't want a candy cane." The boy snatched it from her hand and threw it on the floor. "I want a space gun and I want it now."

"Then I guess you're going to be disappointed," Sherrie said, easing the child off her lap.

The boy stared at her for a second, then opened his mouth and let out a shrill scream. Sherrie looked around in vain for the child's mother, but apparently the woman had taken advantage of the respite from her rebellious child and dashed off to shop.

Sherrie's efforts to calm the child were fruitless. Still yelling, the boy rushed over to the reindeer and, using both fists, began pounding one of them on the head.

"Stop that right now," Sherrie warned, "or Santa won't bring you anything on Christmas Eve."

"Don't want Santa," the boy yelled, aiming a kick at the reindeer's legs. "Santa's stupid."

It was the final straw. Leaping from her chair, she grabbed the squirming child by the arm and hauled him off the platform in front of the waiting customers. Unfortunately his mother arrived on the scene just then, demanding to know why Mrs. Claus was beating up her child.

"He was beating up the reindeer," Sherrie hotly protested. "I was simply removing him from the area."

"Well, you don't remove my child from anywhere," the mother yelled, her voice rising above her son's screams. "That's my job." She was a big woman, and looked as if she could flatten an elephant with one blow.

Sherrie opened her mouth to answer, then closed it again as a deep voice inquired, "What's going on here?"

Sherrie's heart sank as she met the disapproval in Matthew Blanchard's ice blue eyes. She began to explain, but the customer forestalled her.

"I am *never*," she said, pronouncing the word in a voice of doom, "ever setting foot in this store again." She looked around at the line of interested spectators. "If I were you," she added meaningfully, "I'd get out of this store before they all start beating up on your kids."

"Madam—" Matt began, but she cut him off.

Grabbing her son by the hand, she said loudly, "Come on, Henry. We'll find a store where kids are welcome." She glared at Sherrie as she passed. "You should be ashamed of yourself," she snarled. "Posing as Mrs. Claus and then picking on little kids. You should be reported."

Sherrie managed to hold her tongue as the woman led the screaming child away. She flicked a quick glance at Matt, who was addressing the crowd in a calm, quiet tone of reassurance.

"I apologize for this small misunderstanding," he announced. "To make up for the unpleasantness, I'll see that every child in the store gets a free balloon and a candy cane."

He signaled to one of the floorwalkers, a pleasant young man dressed in a red vest and bow tie. "Follow this gentleman," Matt announced, "and he'll hand out the gifts. Meanwhile, Mrs. Claus will take a short break. She'll be back in fifteen minutes."

Sherrie felt a quiver in the region of her stomach. She followed Matt as he threaded his way through the crowd, and rehearsed her defense. He said nothing as led her into his office, but seated himself at his desk and waited for her to stand in front of him.

She felt a spark of resentment when she saw the reprimand in his expression. He was beginning to make her feel like a second-grader hauled up in front of the principal.

"Perhaps, Miss Latimer," he said, his voice heavy with exasperation, "you would be kind enough to explain why you felt it necessary to manhandle one of my valued customers?"

Sherrie lifted her chin. "That valued customer was about to demolish Donna. I felt it necessary to remove the child from the platform to prevent serious damage to the merchandise."

He stared at her for so long she wondered if he'd understood what she'd said. Finally he cleared his throat. "I'm almost afraid to ask," he said, clasping his hands as if in prayer, "but who the devil is Donna?"

"Blitzen's partner, of course."

He looked at her blankly.

"You know," Sherrie said, allowing a tiny note of impatience to enter her voice. "Donna and Blitzen. Santa's reindeer?"

He still looked at her as if she'd suddenly appeared from outer space.

She placed her hands on the desk, leaned forward and pronounced each word as if she were translating a foreign language. "You have two reindeer in your Christmas display. I call them Donna and Blitzen. Had I not removed that brat from the platform, Blitzen would have been looking for a new mate."

A look of apprehension slowly dawned on Matt's face. "I see," he said weakly.

Sensing that she was getting through to him at last, she straightened up. "I didn't hurt the child. He was out of control, and upsetting the other children. I did what I thought was necessary to restore the peace."

Matt nodded. "I sympathize with your predicament, Miss Latimer. It might have been more prudent, however, to have let the child's mother deal with him."

"The child's mother," Sherrie said grimly, "was nowhere to be found. If she can't be bothered to discipline the child, she must learn to accept the consequences. In my opinion, women like that shouldn't have children if they can't accept the responsibility."

She got the feeling she might have said too much as Matt's face darkened. "That's beside the point. We have to remember that our customers are the reason we are in business. Without them, we would not have a Blanchard's Department Store."

"Yes, but—"

"In situations like this," Matt went on firmly, "we must hold on to our temper and do our utmost to soothe ruffled feathers. Throwing the child off the platform was not the best way to handle things, no matter how much he might have deserved it. I must ask you to use more restraint in the future, if you want to keep your job."

It was on the tip of her tongue to tell him where to stuff his job. "I was hired to talk to the children and listen to their Christmas wishes," she said stiffly. "I did not expect to act as nursemaid, baby-sitter or disciplinarian, nor did I expect to be subjected to harassment, ridicule or abuse, all of which has been directed at me in the past two days."

Matt sighed, and leaned back in his chair. "I had an idea the job might be too much for you. If you remember, I did warn you that it was a tough job for a woman. Perhaps I could rustle up a couple of elves to help out."

"In my opinion, Mr. Blanchard, this would be a tough job for that marine sergeant you were looking for." She puffed out her breath. She had promised Tom she would do this job. She would do her best to see it through for his sake, certainly not for the stuffed shirt who sat glowering at her across his too-tidy desk.

Softening her tone with difficulty, she added, "That doesn't mean I can't handle it. There's no need to hire elves. I apologize for losing my patience. I can assure you, it won't happen again."

She waited while he sat in silence, apparently torn by indecision. Miserably she wondered how she was going to explain to Tom that she botched the job after less than two days.

She jumped when Matthew Blanchard suddenly looked up. His eyes looked very blue, and very direct. "Miss Latimer," he said quietly, "everyone around here calls me Matt. I would appreciate it if you would do the same."

She could feel tiny ripples of awareness course down her back. For some reason she really wished she was wearing something other than the frumpy Mrs. Claus costume. She had the distinct feeling that when she spoke, her voice would sound about an octave too high. "Does that mean I'm still Mrs. Claus?"

Matt sighed, as if he had just made an earth-shattering decision. "If you're really sure you want to be harassed and abused for the next month, the job is still yours."

He didn't have to sound quite so enthusiastic about it, Sherrie thought gloomily. If he knew how tough it had been for her to step down and apologize, he wouldn't be nearly so condescending. "I'll manage," she said, her voice deceptively meek. "Thank you, Mr. Blanchard."

"Matt," he reminded her.

Again she felt the shiver of pleasure down her spine. How, she wondered, could he possibly have this effect on her, when she found him so infuriating?

"I think I'd find it easier to call you Matt," she said carefully, "if you'd stop calling me Miss Latimer."

He didn't quite smile, but she had the feeling that one lurked behind the firm line of his mouth. The thought made the ripples travel faster.

"I'll do my best," he murmured. "Now, as long as we've got that settled, you'd better get back to your chair. There's probably a hundred kids waiting for you by now."

"God, I hope not," Sherrie murmured fervently. "By the time Christmas gets here I might not be needing the gray hair. I'll have enough of my own."

She thought she heard him chuckle as she closed the door behind her but she couldn't be sure. She only knew that she would give anything to hear Matthew Blanchard laugh out loud, and to be the one who caused it.

The sooner she started work on her quest for Lucy's mother, the better, she told herself as she walked through the department store. Matthew Blanchard did strange things to her senses.

If he wasn't quite so pompous and patronizing, she might even be tempted to forget her convictions about men in general. And that would be a disastrous mistake. Horrified with her treacherous mind, she hurried back to her seat in the Christmas display.

All that afternoon, when she wasn't chatting to the children, Sherrie racked her brains trying to come up with a suitable candidate for Lucy's mother.

What she really needed, she decided, was more information about Matthew Blanchard. Since he would be a primary factor in the success of her plan, she needed to know what kind of woman might appeal to him.

The line of children had abated and her shift was almost over when Sherrie saw her impervious boss heading in her direction with Lucy in tow. Apparently his daughter was checking up on her request.

Sherrie smiled when the serious little girl climbed onto her lap. The child looked enchanting in a pleated red tartan skirt worn over white tights. The ensemble was completed with a white sweater, decorated with an appliquéd black Scottish terrier. Someone knew how to dress a child, Sherrie thought as she settled the child into the crook of her arm.

"Hello, Lucy," she said, "It's very nice to see you again."

Lucy glanced over at her father, who stood a few feet away, watching his daughter with a worried expression on his face. After a moment's hesitation, Matt stepped up to the platform and said in an urgent voice, "It's pretty quiet out here now. Could you keep an eye on her for a few minutes? I have an important call to make."

Sherrie nodded, wondering what could be important enough to make him leave his daughter in her charge. Considering his opinion of her capabilities, she thought sourly, he was taking quite a chance.

"Did you find a mommy yet?" Lucy asked, after her father strode away.

Sherrie shook her head, hating the disappointment it caused in the child's big blue eyes. "I haven't had much time to look around yet, sweetheart. We are looking for a very special lady, here.''

Lucy dug her hands into her lap. "We just want some-one to love us," she said, in a small voice.

"I know, honey, and I will find that special lady, I promise. But it might take me a little while.''

"Will you find her before Christmas?''

"I'll do my best," Sherrie said warily, "but I can't re-ally promise. It might take me longer than that. You want to be sure we have the right mommy, don't you?''

Lucy nodded. She was silent for a moment or two, then looked earnestly up at Sherrie. "We need a mommy to cook the dinner for Christmas.''

"You do?'' Sherry smiled. "Who usually cooks your dinner?''

"Mrs. Halloway. She lives in our house and cooks the dinner for us.''

Mrs. Halloway was most likely the person who had dressed Lucy in that adorable outfit. Sherrie felt a small twinge of anxiety. Had Matt already chosen his next wife? If so, Lucy obviously wasn't happy about it. "Well, I'm sure Mrs. Halloway can cook you a lovely Christ-mas dinner,'' she said carefully. "Just like a mommy.''

Lucy shook her head so hard her curls bounced. "Mrs. Halloway is too old to be a mommy. She just cleans the house and cooks for us.''

The housekeeper, Sherrie decided, with a rush of re-lief. "Well, I'm sure she'll be happy to cook you a nice dinner for Christmas.''

"She had to go away,'' Lucy said, her gaze shifting to the dazzling Christmas tree behind the chair. "She won't be here for Christmas.''

Now Sherrie could understand the haunted look on Matt's face. "Is she coming back?'' she asked, wondering how Matt was going to manage to take care of the little girl without his housekeeper.

"I dunno." Lucy pointed at the tree. "Who are the presents for?"

"All the children who've been especially good," Sherrie murmured absently. "Don't you have an auntie who can cook for you?"

Lucy shook her head.

"Perhaps Daddy has a nice friend who can take care of you."

Again the blond curls bounced to and fro. "Daddy doesn't have any friends."

Daddy's private life was obviously lacking, Sherrie thought, wondering just how antisocial Matthew Blanchard could be.

"Can you cook dinner?"

The question took Sherrie by surprise. She laughed, and gave the little girl a warm hug. "Of course I can cook. Santa would be very unhappy if he couldn't enjoy his Christmas dinner."

"Can you make pancakes and bacon? And basketty?"

Sherrie raised her eyebrows. "Basketty?"

"You know, those long squiggly things. Mrs. Halloway puts them on a plate an...an...pours red stuff over."

"Spaghetti?" Sherrie suggested, hazarding a guess.

"Yes," Lucy said impatiently. "That's what I said. Basketty."

"I can cook basketty," Sherie said solemnly. "And hamburgers and meat loaf and chocolate cream pie."

"I wish you could come and cook for us," Lucy said, her voice wistful.

Sherrie stared at the little girl. That wasn't such a bad idea. That way she would be right inside the lion's den, so to speak. The perfect place to learn more about Matthew Blanchard. It would be that much easier to introduce him to someone, if she could invite them to his home. Not only that, she wouldn't have to go back to Tom's dreadfully lonely apartment every night.

Of course, she told herself, it would only be temporary, until she found someone suitable for Lucy. In the meantime she could take her time looking around for a new apartment.

In the next instant, she gave herself a mental shake. What on earth was she thinking? First of all, after that fiasco with Henry the Hellion, Matt wasn't likely to trust his daughter to her care full-time. Secondly, she was working at the store until Christmas. She couldn't be in two places at once.

What worried her the most was the excitement she'd felt at the thought of being in the same house as Matthew Blanchard. That was dangerous, and she had better stop this nonsense right away, she told herself.

Not only was Matt way out of her league, but she was also not about to risk having her heart broken again. Not by anyone. Certainly not by a sophisticated, experienced charmer like Matthew Blanchard.

For although he had bent over backward to convince her otherwise, she was quite sure that under the right circumstances, her new boss would be the ultimate in experienced charmers once he set his mind to it. And, much to her dismay, that prospect excited her most of all.

# Chapter Three

Upstairs in his office, Matt threaded his fingers through his hair. Five phone calls, and nothing. There just wasn't anyone out there who was willing to take on the job of a temporary live-in housekeeper. What the hell was he going to do?

He sat there for a moment or two, trying to stem the feeling of panic. He'd have to opt for a baby-sitter, and try to manage the rest himself. Somehow they'd survive until Mrs. Halloway's emergency was over. If she didn't return by Christmas, he'd just have to take Lucy to a restaurant for dinner. The prospect was a gloomy one.

With a start he glanced at the clock. He'd left Lucy down there with Mrs. Claus long enough.

His daughter was still sitting where he'd left her, he discovered when he reached the fifth floor. She looked quite at home in Mrs. Claus's small lap. In fact, something curled inside him when he saw her look up at Sherrie with a big smile spreading over her face.

He hadn't seen Lucy smile like that in a long, long time.

He watched the two of them together for a few moments, touched by the earnest way they were chatting to each other. Lucy had certainly taken to Mrs. Claus. If the rest of the children were as happy with her, this could be the best season yet at Blanchard's.

That had been a brilliant idea of Sherrie Latimer's. He must remember to tell her so when she left. Again that small pang of regret attacked his midriff. Frowning, he shook off the moment of melancholy and strode toward the display.

Lucy's face lit up when she saw her father, and she held out her arms to him.

"Thanks, Mrs. Claus," Matt said gruffly as he scooped his daughter up in his arms. "I appreciate you staying on to watch her for me."

"I enjoyed it," Sherrie said, smiling at him.

For a moment Matt basked in that smile. Now that he knew what she looked like under all that padding, his imagination filled in what he couldn't see. Annoyed with himself for letting his mind stray in that dangerous direction, he gave her a brief nod. "Well, have a good evening. See you tomorrow."

Sherrie watched him leave, Lucy still in his arms. For some reason she felt unutterably lonely. The day was over and she had nothing better to do than go back to that bleak apartment. As well as shop for groceries, she reminded herself as she made her way back to the employees' lounge. Not to mention washing her dress when she got home.

A familiar face greeted her when she entered the lounge.

"Hi, Mrs. Claus," Beryl Robbins said cheerfully. "Survived another day, I see."

Sherrie laughed. "I think I'm growing into the part. My back is permanently bowed and my hair is turning white."

Beryl made a face. "I know what you mean. It's been one of those days. I broke two nails, lost a shipment of Christmas tree ornaments somewhere and Matt got on my case about some kid terrorizing the toy department with one of our bestselling items. I had to pull them all off the shelf. Thank God it's time to go home."

Sherrie studied the woman thoughtfully. She'd offered to answer any questions Sherrie might have. How forthcoming would she be about her boss? Sherrie wondered.

Deciding to find out, she said casually, "I'm going to stop off for a coffee on my way home. If you're not in a hurry, would you care to join me?"

Beryl reached for a brilliant red coat on the coat stand. "Make it an espresso and you've got a deal."

Sherrie grinned. "Just give me time to get out of these clothes and I'll be with you."

The coffee bar was noisy, warm and infinitely better than the empty apartment. Sherrie chose a corner table by the window and waited for her companion to get settled before tackling the subject.

After asking a few questions about the store in general, she slipped in the casual comment. "I met Mr. Blanchard's daughter, Lucy. She seems such a lonely little girl."

Beryl sighed. "I know. It's such a shame. I'm not sure what happened, but as far as I can make out, Matt caught his wife cheating on him and dumped her when Lucy was a year old.''

Sherrie stared at her in dismay. ''He dumped Lucy's mother?''

''Well, I can't say I'm surprised. She was a lot younger than Matt, still a kid herself, really. I heard that she got bored with sitting home alone with a baby while Matt was working. She started going out without him, leaving Lucy with a baby-sitter. She must have been no-good, since Matt got custody.''

''Poor Lucy,'' Sherrie murmured. ''Though it must be hard on her father, too. I don't suppose he has much time to himself, with a daughter to look after.''

''He has a housekeeper who helps take care of Lucy.'' Beryl took a sip of coffee. ''Not that he's much of a party animal. I think he gets out to his health club a couple of times a week. Matt is a strong believer in keeping fit. He tried to start an exercise session at the store, but everyone dropped out after the first week or two. Matt's a tough instructor.''

She could just imagine, Sherrie thought, remembering the broad shoulders and narrow hips of her boss. It took discipline to look that good. She sat up straight, almost spilling her coffee. She had the perfect candidate after all—Elaine Maitland.

Elaine was a secretary at Conway Pharmaceuticals. She was also a fitness freak, not to mention bright, intelligent and attractive. She had made Sherrie feel tired at times, relating her adventures on the ski slopes, the tennis courts and the golf courses, as well as her stints as swim coach for the local grade school and aerobics instructor in her spare time.

Sherrie's idea of exercise was walking around a shopping mall, or an occasional jog across the park on the way to the library.

Having come from a large family, Elaine had often talked about settling down and having a big family herself, if she could only find the right person.

Elaine, Sherrie decided, would be just the right person to be a mother to Lucy and brighten up Matt's life. The only problem now was how to arrange it. That would take some thought.

She tried not to notice the depression she felt at the thought of Matt and Elaine together. She had no wish to get involved with a man again, she reminded herself. At least, not for a long, long time. And if she did, it would not be with anyone like Matthew Blanchard. She was quite certain of that. Almost.

"Why did Mrs. Halloway go 'way?" Lucy demanded as she sat at the kitchen table waiting for Matt to finish cremating the hamburgers.

Standing at the stove, Matt looked at the leathery lumps of ground beef in disgust. "Because her mommy is sick," he murmured, wondering if a large helping of ketchup and mustard would help disguise his lack of culinary expertise.

"Why can't she bring her mommy here?" Lucy sniffed the air with growing suspicion. "What is you cooking?"

"Are. What *are* you cooking." Matt tipped the meat onto a paper towel.

"I'm not cooking," Lucy said, raising her voice in indignation. "You is."

Matt sighed. "I'm cooking hamburgers." He never had any problem cooking on the barbecue. In fact, Mrs. Halloway told him he made the best hamburgers she'd ever tasted. He couldn't understand why cooking them on the stove was so much more difficult.

Opening the door of the microwave, he peered at the frozen fries. They still glistened with frost. Frowning, he shut the door and jabbed at the digital display. Something hummed, and hoping he'd managed to put the oven on this time, he opened the fridge to find some lettuce.

"Well," Lucy said plaintively, "why can't she?"

"Why can't who what?" Matthew asked, his head inside the fridge. The only thing he could find that faintly resembled a head of lettuce was a few dark green leaves that looked suspiciously like spinach.

"Why can't Mrs. Halloway bring her mommy here? Then we could share."

"Mrs. Halloway's mommy is too sick to go anywhere." The microwave beeped three times and Matt gingerly opened the door. This time the fries were steaming. Pleased with himself, he took them out of the oven and piled them on two plates.

"Is it ready yet? I'm hungry."

Matt smiled in triumph. "All ready." Grabbing a bun, he slapped a hamburger between the two halves, shook ketchup on it, squeezed mustard on it, shoved one of the green leaves in it and set it next to the fries.

Carrying the plate to the table he announced hopefully, "You are going to enjoy this, Lucy. Just wait until you taste it."

Lucy looked apprehensive when he set the plate down in front of her. "It's not like the ones Mrs. Halloway makes," she said doubtfully.

"It's better." Matt sat down at the table with his own plate. "Come on, eat it all up and I'll give you some ice cream for dessert."

Lucy took a huge bite out of the bun, and then promptly spit it out. "Don't like it," she said, her look of disgust distorting her face.

Matt took a bite out of his own hamburger and felt like spitting it out, too. "Try the fries," he suggested, without much hope.

"They're wet," Lucy said, touching the soggy potatoes as if they were a pile of worms.

Matt put down his bun. "I've got an idea. Let's just get in the car and go pick up some hamburgers."

Lucy was scrambling down from her chair before he'd finished speaking. Rising to his feet, Matt looked down at the mess on his plate. He could manage everything else pretty well, he thought gloomily. But the one thing he was going to miss the most was Mrs. Halloway's cooking.

Dinners at home were one of the highlights of his day. Not only would it be difficult to replace his housekeeper, as he'd discovered earlier that afternoon, but it would be downright impossible to find someone who could cook as well as Mrs. Halloway.

Matt was busily cleaning the kitchen after they'd returned from the restaurant when Lucy announced, "We can ask Mrs. Claus to cook for us."

Wrestling with the problem of how to get burnt hamburger off the electric rings on the stove, Matt was only half listening. "Good idea," he murmured. "Write her a letter and ask her."

"I don't got to write a letter. I can ask her tomorrow."

Matt paused with the wet sponge in his hand. "Huh?"

"I can ask Mrs. Claus tomorrow. At the store."

"No!" Matt almost shouted. He cleared his throat as Lucy sent him a look of startled surprise. "Er, Lucy, honey, Mrs. Claus has far too much to do. She'd never have the time to cook dinner for us."

"Why not?" Lucy pouted. "Mrs. Halloway does lots of things and she cooked dinner."

"Mrs. Halloway is a housekeeper. She's paid to do those things. Mrs. Claus is a . . . she's a . . ."

"She cooks for Santa," Lucy said, sticking her finger in the melting ice cream on the counter. "She told me. She cooks hamburgers and pancakes and bacon."

Matt's ears pricked up. "Bacon?"

"An' chocolate cream pie an' cookies an' basketty."

"Basketty?"

Lucy licked her finger and grinned. "What's that little pink fishy things that swim on your plate?"

Matt let out a groan of longing. "She cooks shrimp scampi?"

Lucy nodded happily. "She told me."

Matt stared at his daughter for a full two seconds, then shook his head. "No, it'll never work. She's too . . . young."

Lucy uttered a shriek of laughter. "Mrs. Claus is not young. She's really old, like Mrs. Halloway. She's got gray hair and everything."

Again Matt was only half listening. Sherrie Latimer was staying in an empty apartment until after Christmas. She had no other plans. She'd told him as much.

No, it couldn't work. What did she know about taking care of a child? Though he had to admit, he'd admired the way she'd dealt with that brat at the store, even if she had upset his old bat of a mother. Discipline, that's what kids lacked these days.

"Can I, Daddy? Can I?"

Aware of Lucy tugging at his pant leg, he looked down at her. "Can you what, honey?"

"Can I ask Mrs. Claus to cook dinner for us?"

Matt smiled. "We'll see. Now I think it's time you went to bed. If you hurry up and get into your nightgown I'll read you a story."

Half an hour later Matt sank into his favorite armchair feeling as if he'd just worked a double shift at the store. How one tiny little girl could be so exhausting he had no idea. He was used to coming home to a nicely cooked meal, then playing with Lucy until her bedtime while Mrs. Halloway did the dishes.

After that he'd relax with the paper while his housekeeper got his daughter ready for bed, and then he'd read Lucy a story and kiss her good-night, cuddling the sweet-smelling, tidy little girl in her spotless nightgown.

How she'd got that way had been one of the mysteries that he'd taken for granted. Until now.

Bathtime, he'd quickly discovered, was noisy, messy and overwhelmingly strenuous. More tiring than any workout at the health club.

Matt sat up with a groan. Tonight was his health club night. He'd have to give that up while Mrs. Halloway was gone. It was the worst possible time of the year to quit working out. What with all those extra goodies, like Christmas cookies, pies and candy...

He buried his head in his hands. There weren't going to be any Christmas goodies this year. He couldn't even manage a lousy hamburger, let alone Christmas cookies. Of course, he could buy them, but it wouldn't be the same. This year, he was really going to mess up Lucy's Christmas.

Lying awake in his bed that night, Matt turned the problem over in his mind. Where else was he going to find someone to live in until Mrs. Halloway could return? Especially this time of the year?

Nowhere, he answered himself in despair. He'd tried every place in town and a couple out of town. They'd all given him the same answer. He was asking the impossible. There was just no one on their books. Two of the women he'd spoken to had offered him someone part-time in the mornings, no afternoons, no weekends, no cooking. That was the best they could do.

Lucy was in kindergarten until two p.m. He needed someone for when Lucy got home from school.

Which would give Sherrie Latimer time to play her Mrs. Claus role and still be there for Lucy. He could have his daughter dropped off at the store....

Matt groaned aloud. He had to be crazy to even consider the idea. Sherrie Latimer had caused enough trouble in the two days she'd worked for him at the store. What would she do to his household?

Thinking over the fiasco of that evening, he had to admit she couldn't do much worse. Deciding to let matters alone until the morning, he pulled the covers over his head and did his best to forget Mrs. Claus and her sparkling green eyes.

Five minutes later he forced himself to face the real reason he didn't want to invite Sherrie Latimer into his home. He had the distinct feeling that he'd have a tough time ignoring the erotic twinges she stirred up anytime he was within a few feet of her.

If she could unbalance his hormones wearing that ridiculous costume, he could just imagine what she'd do to him wandering around his house in her normal clothes. He did not need that kind of complication.

He had no intention of becoming seriously involved with a woman again, and somehow he doubted that Sherrie Latimer would be interested in anything less than a serious commitment. She had wife and mother written all over her, in spite of her perky smile and seductive mouth.

Matt buried his face in the pillow. How could this be happening to him? It had been four years last September since Lucy's mother had decided she wasn't cut out to be a wife and mother, and had flown off to Europe to "find herself." Lucy had been just one year old. He had sworn then that he would never, ever let a woman devastate him like that again.

Not that he could lay all the blame at Caroline's feet. He should have known she was too young to handle the responsibilities of marriage. The thirteen-year gap in their ages created so many problems. And then there was always some crisis at the store, sometimes taking him well into the night to solve.

More and more, Caroline had been left at home alone with a baby, instead of partying and dancing the way she used to with her friends. Oh, he understood all right. He understood why she became bored, why she resented being tied down, why she fell out of love with him—if she had ever been in love with him.

What he couldn't understand was how she could go off and leave a tiny baby alone with a man who didn't know which end to diaper, let alone how to deal with the hundred and one problems of caring for a small child.

Thank the Lord for housekeepers. He'd been lucky to find a good one, and most of the time it seemed to work. Lucy seemed happy and well-adjusted. It was he who had the problem. Especially at Christmas. That's when he suffered from guilt the most. And this year, unless he did something about it, Christmas was really going to be a bust.

He was caught between a little girl's expectations and his determination to stay away from temptation. And there was only one solution. He would offer Sherrie Latimer the job, and if she accepted, he would let her know where they stood at the earliest opportunity. That way there'd be no room for misunderstandings.

Maybe then he could relax around her instead of seeing her as a threat. After all, it was only for three or four weeks. What could possibly happen in that short time?

Sherrie was ten minutes away from her break the next day when she received a message that Matt wanted to see her in his office. She spent the next ten minutes wondering if Henry the Hellion's mother had sued the store for assault.

By the time she got off the elevator on the top floor, there was a nasty squirming going on in her stomach that couldn't entirely be blamed on the fact that she'd forgotten to grocery shop the day before and had made do with buttered toast for breakfast.

She'd been so busy trying to come up with a way to get Matt and Elaine together, she had completely forgotten the empty cupboards and refrigerator until hunger had forced her into the kitchen. Too tired to go out again, she'd ordered in a pizza.

If she didn't shop on the way home today, she warned herself as she tapped on the door of Matt's office, she'd probably collapse from malnutrition.

Matt's deep voice called out to her, and she edged inside the tastefully furnished room, her padded skirts brushing both sides of the door frame.

He sat behind his desk, tapping a pencil. Sherrie's stomach squirmed even more when she saw his taut features. Something bad must have happened to put that look of desperation on his face. Henry's mother must have sued.

"You wanted to see me, Mr. Blanchard?" she asked warily.

Slowly Matt put the pencil down and looked at her. Sherrie's face was flushed, and her green eyes sparkled like stars on a frosty night. The sudden longing to see her again without all that padding almost took his breath away.

His fingers curled with the effort to control the wild thoughts racing through his head. He opened his mouth to speak, then closed it again.

An expression of alarm spread over Sherrie's face as she stared at him. "There's nothing wrong with Lucy, is there?" she asked anxiously. She stepped closer to the desk and leaned forward on her hands. Her amply padded bosom bumped into a small brass lamp and knocked it over.

Scrambling to right it, she sent a sheaf of papers scattering to the floor. She seemed to have trouble with her padding when she bent down to pick up the papers. Red-faced, she placed them on Matt's desk. "Sorry," she mumbled.

He opened his mouth to answer her, but she chose that moment to adjust her padded bosom with both hands. "I'm just not used to being this plump," she said in a breathy voice that seemed to echo all the way down to his belly.

He could feel tiny beads of sweat forming on his brow. He had to be mad to consider bringing this woman into his home. Every move she made seemed to trigger an erotic response in his body. He wouldn't have a moment's peace.

On the other hand, he wasn't going to get any work done unless someone was taking care of his daughter.

"There's nothing wrong with Lucy," he said in a strangled voice.

Sherrie's face cleared, though her eyes still held a worried look. "It's Henry's mother, then. She sued, right?"

He blinked, trying to think who Henry's mother might be.

"I really didn't hurt him," Sherrie said, sounding defensive.

Something clicked in his brain. Of course, the brat with the loudmouthed mother. "No, nothing like that." He took a deep breath. "I have a proposition for you."

She looked at him as if he were about to suggest she jump out the office window. "What is it?" she asked carefully.

"I need a temporary housekeeper." He couldn't seem to hide the note of resentment in his voice. "Apparently anyone who is remotely qualified is either already employed or on vacation. I was...that is...Lucy and I wondered if you'd be willing to help out until Mrs. Halloway gets back."

She stared at him, her beautiful eyes growing wide. She appeared to be thinking it over. At least, she didn't say anything for a long time. Too long. He realized he'd been holding his breath and let it out in a rush.

"I'd be willing to pay you a generous salary, of course, as well as your room and board," he said, dabbing at his brow with the handkerchief he'd grabbed from his top pocket.

"You want me to live in?"

God, why did everything she say sound like an intimate invitation? While he was still trying to think of an answer, she added warily, "What exactly would the job involve?"

Matt fought to control his voice. "Just take care of my daughter, that's about it. Maybe do a spot of cleaning, wash clothes, that kind of thing." If there was one thing he hated, it was this feeling of being at a disadvantage. Especially with a woman. Even more so with this particular woman.

Making a supreme effort to get back his cool, he sat back in his chair and tapped the edges of his fingers together. "Lucy tells me you can cook," he said, making it sound like a serious requirement for the job.

Sherrie smiled. "I can cook basketty."

Matt nodded. "So I hear. Shrimp scampi, too, I believe."

She looked a little less sure of herself at that, though she sounded confident enough when she said, "I'm sure I could manage just fine. But what about Mrs. Claus?"

"Well, if you could manage both jobs . . ."

She thought about it while he watched her anxiously. After a moment or two, she nodded. "I'd like to give it a try."

Matt let out his breath once more. "I really appreciate that, Miss . . . er . . . Sherrie. Could you move in today? I know it's short notice, but—"

"I think I can do that."

"Good." His relief at having solved his problem was offset by the strong conviction he was creating another. It was a matter of the lesser of two evils. If he couldn't ignore his primitive instincts for a month then he wasn't the man he thought he was, he told himself, without much assurance.

He sat straight in his chair. "I've arranged for the kindergarten bus driver to drop Lucy off at the store," he told Sherrie, who, judging by her expression, was beginning to have her own doubts about her new job. "She should get here shortly before your shift is over. I'll keep her in the office until you're ready to pick her up, then you can take her home. There's just one thing . . ."

He hesitated, while Sherrie waited, apparently wondering what else he was going to spring on her. "I'd rather Lucy didn't know that you are Mrs. Claus," he said at last. "I don't want to destroy the illusion . . . you know . . . the Santa Claus thing . . ."

"Of course." She smiled warmly at him. "Don't worry, Lucy will never know about my secret life as Mrs. Claus."

Once more he had trouble concentrating. Her smile could do the damnedest things to his body. He hastily dropped his gaze and reached for his notepad. Scribbling down his address, he murmured, "This is where I live. Are you familiar with the area?"

He tore the page off and gave it to her. She studied it for a moment, then nodded. "I'll find it. I have to go home first and pick up a few things."

"Of course. You can take Lucy with you." He reached for the ring of keys lying in the ashtray and took one off. "Here, I'll give you a key to the house." His sense of impending doom deepened as her slim fingers took the key from him.

"Thanks," he said as she slipped it with the address into her pocket. "I really appreciate this."

"It will be fun," she assured him. "I'll come up here for Lucy as soon as I change out of my costume."

"Fine, fine." Matt nodded. "That'll be fine." All he could think about was the fact that at last he was going to see her without that lumpy costume again.

She was almost through the door when he thought to add, "You can cook Christmas cookies, can't you?"

She grinned at him over her shoulder. "That's one thing I do know how to make."

He was still dealing with that grin when she closed the door.

Before she went back to the Christmas display, Sherrie took a moment to put a call through to Conway Pharmaceuticals. This new development was going to make her quest for Lucy's mom that much easier, she thought with rising excitement as she dialed the number. It was one of the reasons she'd jumped at it.

That and the fact that she wouldn't have to spend Christmas alone in Tom's depressing apartment, she assured herself. The thought of seeing a lot of Matthew Blanchard had nothing to do with it, of course.

After waiting a minute or two, she heard Elaine's lilting voice on the line. The secretary sounded rather subdued when she said, "Sherrie? I'm so sorry about what happened. I can imagine how you must feel."

Sherrie drew in a sharp breath. Elaine had been one of the guests at her wedding—her almost wedding. Although she'd been prepared, the note of sympathy brought back the pain for a brief moment. "It was for the best," she said, delivering her stock answer. "Now I'm just going to put it all behind me."

"Of course. If there's anything I can do..."

"As a matter of fact there is. I need a favor."

Elaine's voice became wary. "Oh, well, if I can..."

"I need some papers from my desk," Sherrie said firmly. "I won't be back until after the New Year and I need to do some work on them. I was wondering if you'd mind dropping them off for me on your way home?"

She held her breath through the long pause at the end of the line. Then Elaine said doubtfully, "Well, I suppose I could. Are you still in your apartment?"

Sherrie gave her the new address, smiling at the surprise in Elaine's voice when she said, "Oh, I know where that is. I had no idea you were living there."

"Actually I'm doing a favor for a friend. I'll tell you all about it when I see you." Quickly Sherrie explained what papers she needed, then thanked Elaine and hung up before the secretary could change her mind.

Well pleased with her success, she made her way back to the fifth floor. All she had to do now was make sure that she kept Elaine at the house until Matt got there. Then she'd find some way to leave them alone together.

The thought of that swept away all her excitement. It was hard to think of Matt and Elaine together. But necessary, she assured herself a moment later. And she had no business brooding over it. Lucy needed a mom, so Matt had to have a wife. She just hoped she was doing the right thing.

# Chapter Four

Sherrie was surprised when she saw Matt striding toward her later that afternoon with Lucy at his side. She wondered for a moment if he'd changed his mind about hiring her as his housekeeper. She realized she'd be terribly disappointed if he had. She was relieved when he explained that Lucy had insisted on visiting Mrs. Claus again.

"I suspect this visit is going to be a daily event," he said, giving Sherrie a warning glance that she immediately interpreted. It wouldn't be easy keeping her two roles separate while she was with the little girl, but she would have to do her best to see that Lucy's faith in Santa was not destroyed.

Lucy was bursting to tell her something, Sherrie could tell. "We're going to get a new housekeeper," she announced when Sherrie asked her about her day. "I wanted to ask you to cook for us but Daddy said you're too busy."

"I'm afraid I am," Sherrie said gravely. "I have so many children to talk to and listen to their wishes. But I know you'll like the new housekeeper."

"Did you send her?" Lucy demanded.

Sherrie sent Matt a quick glance, but he was watching two little girls arguing over a miniature oven in the toy department. "Yes, I did," she said, deciding it wouldn't hurt. "I wanted to make sure you had a nice house-keeper."

Lucy thought about it for a little while. "Is she going to be my new mommy?"

Sherrie's heart gave an unexpected sharp tug. "No, sweetheart, she isn't. But she might be able to help find one for you."

"I hope so," Lucy said earnestly. "I need one soon."

Sherrie had to agree. Matt must have dressed the child that morning. Only a man would team an orange sweat-shirt with shocking pink pants. The sweatshirt was on backward, as well, she noticed.

After promising Lucy that she would try even harder to make her wish come true, Sherrie watched the little girl run to her father. He smiled down at her as he took her hand and led her away. Sherrie watched them go, wondering how it would feel if a man like Matthew Blanchard smiled at her like that.

Matt was at his desk, helping Lucy color a Christmas tree, when he heard the light tap on his door. "Come in," he called out, without looking up. He was attempting to fill in the toy soldier's hat without going over the line. Lucy tended to get critical if he crossed over the line.

"Mr. Blanchard? I've come to pick up Lucy."

"It's Matt, remember?" He poised the crayon over the delicate peak of the cap and glanced up.

It had been a while since he'd seen her in street clothes. Today she wore a figure-hugging pink top over a black-and-white checkered skirt. Nobody should look that good in everyday clothes, he thought, his eyes glazing over as he took in the glorious picture of Sherrie Latimer smiling at him.

"Daddy, you went outside the line!"

Aware that he'd been staring at his new employee, Matt looked hastily down at the coloring book. Somehow his crayon had wandered across the soldier's face, giving him a lopsided mustache.

Matt snapped the book shut. "Lucy..." His voice cracked and he cleared his throat and tried again. "Lucy, this is Miss Latimer...er...Sherrie. She is going to help out at the house until Mrs. Halloway gets back."

Lucy studied the exquisite face of Sherrie Latimer for a long moment. "You don't look like a housekeeper," she said finally.

Matt was forced to agree. "Sherrie isn't really a housekeeper," he said, doing his best to avoid looking at the transformed Mrs. Claus, "she is just going to help us out for a little while. She's even going to cook dinner for us."

Lucy's face brightened. "Can you make basketty?"

Sherrie laughed, dazzling Matt again for a heated moment. "Of course I can, sweetheart. Would you like some tonight?"

Lucy frowned. "You sound like Mrs. Claus."

Matt snapped out of his daze. The last thing he wanted to do was destroy Lucy's Christmas fantasy.

"Do I?" Sherrie bent her knees and squatted down in front of the little girl. "That's probably because Mrs. Claus sent me to help you. I don't look like her though, do I?"

"No." Once more Lucy studied Sherrie's face while Matt held his breath. Finally the little girl smiled. "Mrs. Claus told me she was going to send you."

"She told me what a wonderful little girl you are," Sherrie said softly. "I'm very happy to meet you, Lucy."

Lucy grinned happily. "Can we have basketty tonight?"

"You bet, sweetheart. How would you like to come with me to my house to get some clothes, then we can go home to your house and you can show me all your toys."

Lucy enthusiastically agreed.

Now that the danger was over, Matt noticed that Sherrie's skirt had slipped up an inch or two from her bent knees. He made a supreme effort to drag his gaze away from the intriguing glimpse of well-shaped thighs and concentrated on his daughter instead.

Lucy seemed quite happy with the new arrangement, and appeared to have taken to Sherrie right away. Maybe things were going to work out all right after all, Matt thought. He felt his shoulders begin to relax for the first time since Mrs. Halloway had given him the distressing news that her mother was ill and she had to fly to California to take care of her.

"What time do you think you'll be home, Matt?" Sherrie asked as she led Lucy to the door. "I'd like to know when to plan dinner."

For a moment he was mesmerized by the way his name sounded on her lips. As far as he could remember, it was the first time she'd actually used it. Then he realized that both she and Lucy were staring at him, waiting for his answer.

He picked up a pencil and began tapping it on the desk. "Er... I should be home around ... six?"

Sherrie nodded. "I'll plan dinner for six-thirty. That will give you time to relax before you eat."

"Daddy likes basketty, too, don't you, Daddy?" Lucy said happily.

Matt did his best to look as enthusiastic as his daughter. "Of course I do. Now go with Sherrie and I'll see you when I get home."

"Can we go an' see Mrs. Claus?" Lucy asked as they went out the door.

Matt closed his eyes as he heard Sherrie explaining that Mrs. Claus had to go home, too. Knowing his daughter, she wouldn't leave it at that. She'd want to know all the details. He just hoped Sherrie would be able to handle it.

Lucy was growing up so fast, he thought sadly. Next year she'd be in grade school, and no doubt some smart kid would tell her that there was no Santa Claus—and no Mrs. Claus. This could be the last year that she believed, and he wanted her to keep the fantasy for as long as possible. Just one last year, he prayed silently, as the door closed behind his small daughter. Just one last year.

Pulling her car up to Matt's driveway later, Sherrie gazed at the house with approval. Built halfway up a hill, it stood in the midst of elegant homes spaced far enough apart to provide a decent-size yard. The front windows of the house overlooked the river, and towering fir trees lined the fenced backyard.

In spite of the rainy darkness, Sherrie could see the outline of a large swing set planted in the middle of a well-kept lawn as she parked her car in the driveway.

She could hardly wait to see the inside. The house breathed opulence. Opening the front door, she found the light switch and turned it on.

Light dazzled her from a crystal chandelier hanging
over the marble entry. To her right a wide, curving stair-
case carpeted in rich maroon led to the top floor, while
on the left several doors led off a paneled hallway.

She caught a glimpse of a spacious living room and
formal dining room as she followed Lucy down the hallway to the enormous kitchen. At least it seemed huge after the tiny cubicle in Tom's apartment.

Sherrie was thankful to see a row of cookbooks standing on a shelf by the stove. She was an average cook at
best. Shrimp scampi, for instance, was something she'd
seen only on a restaurant menu. Lucy had stretched the
truth a little there.

She wondered if Elaine could make the dish. She would
have to mention the fact that it was one of Matt's favorite meals, if the look on his face when he'd mentioned it
was anything to go by.

At least she could manage spaghetti and meatballs, she
thought as she checked out the cupboards. That, at least,
should present no problem. She'd worry about the rest
tomorrow.

Unlike Tom's meager food supply, Matt's housekeeper kept an impressive array of packages and bottles
in her cupboards. The variety of spices and herbs on one
of the shelves made Sherrie nervous. She could be in
trouble from the start. Mrs. Halloway was apparently an
excellent cook. She'd be a tough act to follow.

Lucy was impatient to show Sherrie her bedroom, and
insisted on bringing out every doll, book and game, until Sherrie laughingly protested that she had to prepare
dinner.

She barely had time to get her coat off and familiarize
herself with the rest of the house before she heard the
slam of a car door outside. For a moment her heart

skipped in anticipation when she thought it might be Matt, but then the doorbell rang.

Lucy ran to the door and reached up with both hands to turn the handle. Suddenly tongue-tied, she stared up at the tall, willowy woman who stood on the doorstep.

"Elaine!" Sherrie opened the door wider. "Thanks so much for stopping by. Come in out of that rain."

Elaine eyed Lucy curiously as she stepped inside the door and shook out her umbrella. Opening her briefcase, she took out a file and handed it to Sherrie. "I hope I got the right one."

Sherrie glanced at it. "Perfect. Thanks a lot, Elaine."

"So, what are you doing in this place?" Elaine asked, glancing at the wide sweep of the carpeted stairway. "Isn't this a little out of your league?"

"Very." Sherrie quickly explained about the temporary housekeeping job, then introduced Lucy, who managed a shy smile. "Come on in to the kitchen," she added, leading the child down the hallway. "I'll make you a cup of coffee."

Elaine started to protest but Sherrie pretended not to hear her. Inside the warmth of the kitchen, she insisted that Elaine sit at the breakfast bar. Reluctantly the secretary slipped out of her raincoat.

Sherrie took it from her and went back into the hallway to hang it up in the closet. She came back just in time to hear Lucy ask timidly, "Are you going to be my new mommy?"

"No, sweetheart," Sherrie said hastily as Elaine raised her eyebrows. "Elaine just came to bring some papers for me."

Lucy apparently lost interest. "I'm going to watch TV," she announced, and headed out the door toward the living room.

"What was all that about?" Elaine asked, sitting herself down at the breakfast bar. "What happened to her mother?"

Sherrie measured coffee into the machine. "I'm not sure," she said, reluctant to repeat what she'd heard from Beryl. "I know Lucy hasn't seen her since she was a baby."

"What's her father like?" Elaine crossed her long, slim legs. Her dark hair, with its cute pixie cut, accentuated her high cheekbones and pert nose. She wore an elegant black-and-white dress, and huge black hoops dangled from her ears. She looked sophisticated, confident and quite at home in Matt's kitchen.

Sherrie ignored the tiny pang of envy. This was the kind of woman Matt needed. A companion with the same interests and outlook on life. A woman who could take care of Matt's child and his home with organized efficiency, a trait that Sherrie had never been able to achieve.

"He's very nice, actually," she said, answering Elaine's question. "Charming, considerate and very capable. He's also physically active, and spends a lot of time at the health club."

"And well-heeled, apparently," Elaine murmured, looking around the designer kitchen. "What does he do for a living?"

Sherrie told her, watching her friend's face light up when she mentioned Blanchard's. "He's quite good-looking, too," she threw in for good measure.

Elaine eyed her suspiciously. "There has to be something wrong with him, otherwise some enterprising woman would have snapped him up by now. What about you? You're not being caught on the rebound are you?"

"Of course not," Sherrie said with an emphatic toss of her head. "I'm not in the least bit interested in him in that way. Or any man for that matter."

"I don't blame you," Elaine murmured. "I don't think I would be, either, after what happened to you."

"Matt just doesn't think he needs a wife," Sherrie said, steering the conversation back on track. "Or that Lucy needs a mother. I guess it's up to the right woman to convince him otherwise."

Elaine looked as if she thought that was extremely doubtful.

Sherrie glanced at the clock. It was five past six. Matt should be home at any minute. She poured out the coffee and handed a steaming cup to her friend. For several minutes she kept Elaine chatting about the latest developments at work. "What are you doing for dinner?" she asked impulsively, as Elaine drained her cup. "I'm only cooking spaghetti and meatballs, but you're welcome to stay, if you don't mind eating in the kitchen. I hate eating alone, and I'd enjoy the company."

Elaine looked surprised. "You're not eating with the family?"

"I don't think housekeepers eat with their employers," Sherrie said, opening a cabinet to look for the spaghetti.

"That doesn't seem right to me. I mean, if you go to all the trouble to cook for them, you should at least be able to eat with them. It's not as if you're their permanent housekeeper."

"I'm still employed by Matt. I wouldn't feel right about eating with them."

"Well, I know I wouldn't want to be stuck in the kitchen eating all by myself."

Elaine slid off the bar stool, and Sherrie looked at her in dismay. "You're not leaving already? I thought you were staying for dinner."

"Well, thanks for the invitation, but I think I'd better be getting home. My cat will be wondering where I am—" She broke off as the sound of the front door opening echoed down the hallway.

"That's probably Matt now," Sherrie said, when the door closed again with a loud thud. "Come and meet him."

"Oh, I don't think—" Elaine began, but Sherrie was already opening the kitchen door.

"Hi, Matt!" she called out cheerfully. Her heart thumped at the sight of him. He wore the collar of his raincoat turned up and the wind had tousled his hair. He looked far more approachable now that he was away from the office, and his magnetic presence right there in the hallway of his own home unsettled her more than she cared to admit.

He halted at the doorway to the living room, from where loud clatters and bangs suggested that Lucy was watching cartoons.

Before he could speak, Sherrie said hurriedly, "I've just made coffee, if you'd like a cup?"

He hesitated, glancing at the living-room door.

"I'd like you to meet a friend of mine." She tried to put some enthusiasm in her voice. "She's just on her way out, but she wanted to meet you before she left."

Matt looked taken aback, and behind her Sherrie heard Elaine draw in a sharp breath.

"She's right here," Sherrie said, opening the door wider.

Matt came forward slowly, as if his feet were taking him somewhere he didn't want to go.

Elaine stood by the bar, waiting with a look of apprehension. Her face smoothed out into a smile, however, when she got a good look at Matt. Gliding toward him, she held out an elegantly poised hand. "Mr. Blanchard, how nice to meet you. I'm Sherrie's friend, Elaine Maitland. She's told me so much about you."

Matt shot a startled look at Sherrie and then grasped Elaine's hand and gave it a decisive shake. "Nice to meet you, Miss Maitland."

"Elaine was kind enough to bring me some important papers from work," Sherrie said, indicating the file she'd laid on the table. "I thought I should at least offer her coffee."

"Of course," Matt murmured politely. "It's a dismal night out there."

Elaine nodded in agreement. "It's miserable. I hate having to go home alone to a dark, cold, empty apartment."

"Oh, so do I," Sherrie said emphatically. "I know what it's like, living alone. There's no one at home to make you welcome."

"Except the cat." Elaine gave Matt a dazzling smile. "She does her best but I have to admit, the conversation's rather limited."

Matt looked confused.

"I was going to ask you if you'd mind if Elaine stayed for dinner," Sherrie said, grasping at this slim opportunity. "But she has to go home to feed the cat."

"Oh, well, perhaps I could stay for an hour or two." Elaine smiled at Matt. "You have a very nice home, Mr. Blanchard. I'd really love to see the rest of it."

Matt's eyebrow twitched at this not very subtle suggestion. "I'm sure Sherrie will be happy to show you around." He looked meaningfully at Sherrie. "That's if she can find her way."

"Well, actually, Lucy did show me most of it, but right now I have to get dinner." Sherrie marched behind the bar and began opening cabinets with a display of urgency.

"In that case, I'll do the honors," Matt said reluctantly. He turned to Elaine and gave her a charming smile that would have caused a meltdown in Sherrie's body had it been directed at her. "Have you met my daughter, Miss Maitland?"

"Oh, do call me Elaine." She tucked her hand possessively into his arm. "You don't mind if I call you Matt, do you? As for your lovely little daughter, she's an absolute doll." She gave Sherrie a knowing little grin.

Matt looked uncomfortable at this display of familiarity, but gamely led Elaine to the door.

"See you later," Elaine gleefully called out as she disappeared from view.

Sherrie let out her breath. So far, so good. She'd bought some time and managed to get them all together for a little while, at least. Now Matt could see how Elaine and Lucy reacted to each other. She only hoped that Lucy would open up to the energetic secretary the way she did with Mrs. Claus.

She did her best to ignore the ache in her heart that wouldn't seem to go away. She was still feeling the pangs of her broken engagement, she told herself. Though she hadn't given Jason much thought in quite a while. In fact, now that she really thought about it, she could look back on the whole mess as a blessing in disguise.

She'd met Jason when she'd spilled her tub of popcorn all over him in the movie theater. They were both there alone, and he'd walked her home after the movie.

They started dating, and although she had trouble understanding Jason's moods and long silences, she loved his dry humor and their deep discussions on the meaning of life, even if she hadn't fully understood them.

He proposed, not very romantically, on Christmas Eve, after a cozy dinner in front of the fire in her apartment. She was truly surprised, but caught up in the festive mood, she laughingly accepted. The doubts came soon after, when Jason seemed reluctant to discuss wedding plans.

She began to see how different they were, how little they had in common. Finally, when she told him she'd decided to break up with him, he suggested a Thanksgiving wedding. Afraid she might be throwing away her future happiness, she agreed.

As the day drew nearer, Jason grew more and more withdrawn. He broke dates without notice, then pretended nothing had happened. When she questioned him, he assured her he still loved her and wanted to marry her.

She ignored her doubts as she waited for him at the church. She loved him, she told herself, and she'd make it work. Then Paul, his best man, had arrived, and as gently as possible, had told her that Jason had changed his mind. He'd sent Paul to tell her that he wasn't ready to marry her yet. He was leaving town to explore new possibilities.

She and Jason would never have been happy together, she knew that now. Though what it was exactly that had made her see the light she couldn't imagine.

Unable to find any frozen meatballs in the freezer, Sherrie had to set to and make them from scratch. After defrosting the ground meat in the microwave and a lot of measuring and mixing, she studied the finished meatballs with a dubious frown. They didn't look much like the perfectly formed ones she always bought from the freezer case. They were odd shapes and sizes, and she had an idea she'd overdone it a bit with the spices, but all in all, she decided, they weren't bad for a first effort.

Matt had returned with Elaine to the living room by the time Sherrie announced dinner was ready. They had sat down together on the couch, and Matt appeared to be listening attentively to Elaine's rapid-fire account of the daring rescue she'd made in the swimming pool last summer.

Lucy was ignoring them both, her attention fixed firmly on the blaring television set with which Elaine was valiantly competing.

Throwing caution to the wind, Sherrie had laid three places at the long oak table in the dining room, and lit the tall, white candles that stood in the brass centerpiece. Now Matt could hardly refuse to allow Elaine to eat with them.

For a moment she thought he was going to do just that as he stared at the place settings. Then he looked at her with a quizzical expression that caused a flutter or two beneath her breast. "I believe there are four of us," he said succinctly.

She knew that, she thought irritably. She'd much rather be eating at the table with him. "I have to serve the meal," she said, aware that she sounded put-upon.

"We're having spaghetti and meatballs," Matt said, raising his eyebrows. "How long does it take to serve that?"

"I have salad, as well," Sherrie said, weakening.

"I want Sherrie to sit with me," Lucy announced.

"Of course you must sit with us, Sherrie," Elaine said, in a proprietary tone that Sherrie found somewhat offensive.

"I guess it's unanimous, then." Matt gave Elaine a smile of conspiracy, making Sherrie clench her teeth.

She wasn't sure how badly she wanted to sit there and watch the two of them getting to know each other. In fact, now that she could see them together, she wasn't at all sure she'd made the right choice. Elaine seemed just a tiny bit superficial, and she'd paid hardly any attention to Lucy, for whom Sherrie had gone to all this trouble.

"I'll get the spaghetti," she said, and reluctantly left them alone again. She made an effort to cool her resentment as she opened the door of the fridge. She couldn't imagine why she was getting so upset. It had to be nerves making her so edgy.

After all, her plan seemed to be going well enough as far as Matt was concerned. Elaine was obviously thrilled about meeting him, and he seemed to be enjoying her company.

Lucy didn't seem too enthusiastic, but then, she hadn't had time to get used to Elaine, that was all. Which wasn't surprising, Sherrie thought, as she snatched the bowl of salad from the shelf, since Elaine appeared to be so wrapped up in Matt she'd hardly spoken a word to the child.

She jumped violently when a large hand prevented her from closing the fridge door.

"I thought we'd have a bottle of wine with dinner," Matt said, in his deep voice. "It should be red, I suppose, but I prefer white."

Having him stand so close to her made her nervous. She prayed she wouldn't drop the salad as she peered into the fridge again. "There's two bottles in the back. One's a chardonnay, I think."

"Let me take a look."

She stood back to let him look inside the fridge. As he stooped down next to her she recognized the faint, spicy fragrance of his expensive cologne. It reminded her of the man who wore it—spicy, with a touch of sophistication, and disturbingly masculine.

He'd taken off his suit jacket, though he still wore his tie with a crisp, blue striped shirt. The fabric stretched across his wide shoulders, and she could see the muscles flex as he reached into the fridge for the bottle.

She couldn't help noticing how his dark hair curled slightly above the collar. The urge to run her fingers through it almost overwhelmed her.

She watched him straighten up, the bottle of wine in his hand. Still preoccupied, she noticed that his stomach looked quite flat above the belt of his pants. The workouts at the health club had kept him in really good shape.

She hadn't realized that the fridge door had closed until the sudden tense silence jarred her senses. Aware that she'd been staring where she shouldn't, she felt her cheeks growing warm.

Keeping her gaze firmly fixed on the salad in her arms, she muttered, "I'll take this into the dining room."

His voice sounded a little strained when he answered, "I'll bring in the spaghetti."

She nodded her thanks and fled from the kitchen.

Lucy was telling Elaine all about Mrs. Claus when Sherrie got back to the dining room. Thankful that she hadn't mentioned that part of the deal to Elaine, she waited for Matt to put the dish of spaghetti down in the middle of the table.

"I adore spaghetti," Elaine said, fluttering her eyelashes at him. "In fact, Italian food is my very favorite. Do you like to eat Italian, Matt?"

Right then he didn't look as if he liked to eat anything, Sherrie thought as she watched him move around to his chair.

"Yes, I do, very much," he said as he sat down. "Though I have to admit, I enjoy any kind of good food."

"Ah," Elaine murmured, looking deep into his eyes. "A gourmet. How interesting. I happen to know this darling little restaurant on the edge of town—"

"Excuse me," Matt said, getting up again, "I have to dish up Lucy's dinner."

"Oh, I'll do that," Sherrie said, reaching for a plate.

Matt seemed to hover uneasily for a moment or two, then reluctantly sat down.

Elaine laid her hand on his arm. "I must tell you about the bike ride I took through the Cascade Mountains," she said. "You'll love this."

She launched into a lively account of her harrowing ride, while Sherrie piled spaghetti onto Lucy's plate.

"This is my very favorite dinner," Lucy said, licking her lips as she gazed at her plate.

"Mine, too," Sherrie said, trying not to notice how annoying Elaine's giggle had become.

Even Matt's eyes seemed to glaze over, she observed, as he speared a meatball and popped it into his mouth.

Lucy sucked in a long strand of spaghetti with a loud slurping noise. Sherrie took the fork from the child's hand and showed her how to wrap the strands around the prongs with her spoon.

"This tastes better'n Mrs. Halloway makes," Lucy announced, chomping happily on a mouthful of pasta.

Matt's voice sounded a little hoarse when he asked Sherrie if she wanted a glass of wine.

Sherrie shook her head. She couldn't drink more than a glass of wine without it going to her head, and she needed to be in full command of her senses. Something told her that she had made a bad mistake, and she wasn't sure what to do about it.

Elaine seemed to be doing all the talking, while Matt had hardly said a word. In fact, the longer she saw them together, the more Sherrie was convinced that they were not a good match.

"I'm going on a cross-country ski run this weekend," Elaine said, sifting through her spaghetti with her fork. "How would you like to join me, Matt?" She seemed to be leaving all the meatballs on her plate, Sherrie noticed.

"I'm afraid I don't have much leisure time," Matt said, reaching for his wine. "Especially this time of year. The store keeps me busy and I like to spend what spare time I have with Lucy."

"Oh, well, she could come, too," Elaine said, her voice notably lacking enthusiasm.

"I don't think that would be a good idea." Matt took a sip of wine and put down his glass. "Thank you for the invitation, though."

Sherrie took her first bite of meatball and almost gasped. She must have misjudged the spice. They were the hottest meatballs she'd ever tasted. She glanced over at Lucy, who appeared to be enjoying her dinner, in spite of her red, watery eyes.

"Well," Elaine said, "I heard about this cool, new nightclub that's just opened up on Third Street. The Marrakesh, I think it's called. They have a hot rock band with wonderful strobe lights and laser effects. I'd love to take you dancing there, to thank you for this wonderful dinner."

Cooked by her, Sherrie thought, her resentment growing.

"I'm afraid I'm not that good a dancer," Matt said, beginning to look uncomfortable.

"I could teach you." Elaine patted his arm. "Come on, you'll enjoy it. Sherrie can take care of Lucy. It will be a nice break for you."

Matt's face seemed to close up. "I'm really not interested in going to nightclubs." He looked at his watch. "Now, if you will excuse me, I have some work to do in my office."

He signaled Sherrie with his eyes. "It's time Lucy was getting ready for bed," he said pointedly. "If you'll bathe her, I'll come up and read her a story before she goes to sleep."

Sherrie's heart gave an uncomfortable thump. She had forgotten all about Matt's ex-wife, until now. Elaine probably reminded him of her—the young bride who'd become bored with married life, and wrecked their marriage.

Elaine had been a bad choice. She was too young, only a year older than Sherrie herself. Matt didn't need a frivolous, self-centered party animal like Elaine. He needed someone mature, someone sensible, someone reliable. He needed someone he could relax with, someone who would be quite happy to stay home and take care of him and his daughter.

She'd messed things up again, as usual, Sherrie thought miserably. She'd let Lucy down, and she'd managed to upset Matt on her first night in his home. It was not a good beginning.

# Chapter Five

Sherrie watched Matt politely bid Elaine good-night, and then he left the room. Lucy got up from the table and ran after him, and Sherrie stood to collect the dishes.

"What an odd man," Elaine said, obviously affronted by Matt's rejection. "No wonder his wife left him."

"His wife left him because she was too immature to think about anyone but herself," Sherrie said shortly.

Elaine raised an eyebrow. "Well, don't get on my case. I was only trying to be friendly to the man. He's too much of a stuffed shirt for my taste, anyway." She pushed herself away from the table. "I have to get home, before my cat starves to death."

Sherrie went with her to the front door, thanking her again for bringing the papers by.

Elaine pulled on her raincoat, and picked up her umbrella. "If you want my advice," she said, stepping out into the cold, damp night, "you'll find another way to spend your vacation. You shouldn't be burying yourself in this big house all alone. Why don't you go to one of those singles resorts for the holidays? After all, the best cure for a man is another man."

"The last thing I want is another man," Sherrie said grimly. "Besides, I'm not alone. I have plenty to keep me busy taking care of Matt and Lucy."

Elaine sniffed, as if she considered that poor company. "You'll change your mind soon enough. The holidays can be terribly depressing when you're lonely."

Closing the door behind her friend, Sherrie leaned against it with a sigh. Her first attempt had been a miserable failure. She would have to be much more careful about whom she picked for Lucy's mother. She couldn't afford another mistake.

She found Lucy in the living room with her father when she went in search of her. The child was leaning over Matt's arm while he read the comic strips to her from the newspaper.

"I'm sorry about Elaine," Sherrie said, when they both looked up as she entered the room. "I hope you don't mind me suggesting she stay for dinner."

"Not at all," Matt said evenly. "You're welcome to invite whomever you like, though I'm afraid I'd have to draw the line at a wild and crazy party."

Sherrie gave him a tired smile. "Wild parties are not my thing, so you don't have to worry about that." She held out her hand to Lucy. "Come on, sweetheart, let's go find a toy to play with in the tub."

Lucy ran to her and grasped her hand. "Can I take my teddy bear for a swim?"

"I don't think teddy bears can swim," Sherrie said, leading the little girl to the door. "But I'm sure we'll find something that can."

She wasn't sure, but she thought she heard Matt sigh as he rattled the newspaper behind her.

Stacking dishes into the dishwasher later, she struggled with the problem of who to choose for her next candidate. None of her single friends seemed to fit the bill. They were all too immature, too irresponsible or too independent to take on a ready-made family. She could see that now.

What she needed was an older woman. The problem was, all the older women she knew were already married.

Concentrating on the problem, Sherrie held a plate under the faucet and slowly rinsed it off. She didn't hear Matt enter the kitchen until he spoke right behind her.

"You must be dead on your feet," he said quietly.

She spun around, spraying water from the plate over his shirt. "Oh, darn, I'm sorry." Grabbing a paper towel, she dabbed at the wet fabric.

He flinched as she touched him, then stilled her hand with his. "Don't worry about it. The shirt's going into the wash, anyway." For a brief moment his fingers trapped hers against his stomach, then he let her go.

Sherrie felt tiny shock waves from his touch shoot all the way up her arm. Afraid he would notice the upheaval he'd caused, she turned back to the sink, mumbling, "My brother is always teasing me about my clumsiness."

"Most people are clumsy when they're tired."

Trying to recover her composure, she said unsteadily, "I must be constantly tired, then." She stacked the last plate into the dishwasher and closed the door. "Is Lucy asleep?"

"She wanted to say good-night to you. That's what I came to tell you."

Sherrie dried her hands on the kitchen towel she'd hung over the oven door. "I'll go up right away."

He stood in her way, but made no effort to move. "I saw your bags in the hallway," he said, thrusting his hands into the pockets of his slacks. "I took them up to your room for you."

"Oh, thank you." Her heart skipped crazily at the thought of sleeping in the room next to his, and she had trouble meeting his gaze. The light played across his face, gentling his harsh features, while intensifying the clear blue of his eyes.

She saw a tiny indentation at the corner of his mouth, and wondered why she hadn't noticed it before. Standing this close to him in the quiet intimacy of his kitchen was definitely bad for her peace of mind, she decided.

He seemed so different from the stern store owner seated behind that big, impressive desk in his office. If she'd known he was going to unsettle her this much, she would have thought twice about agreeing to fill in for his housekeeper.

This man was dangerous. Not only could he make her forget her good intentions, putting her heart in jeopardy again, but he could sabotage her efforts to grant Lucy her wish.

"Did Lucy show you the guest room?" he asked as she tried to think of something intelligent to say.

"Yes, thank you." She edged over to the door. "Well, I guess I should say good-night to Lucy."

"Before you go," Matt said, "there's something I want to say to you."

Her heart sank. Apparently she was going to get a lecture after all. He'd waited until Lucy had gone to bed, rather than chastise her in front of the child.

She met his gaze squarely, determined not to let him upset her. Though he didn't look mad. In fact, she thought, with a leap of her pulse, he was looking at her as if he was concerned about her for some reason.

"Thank you for a nice dinner," he said quietly.

She let out an unsteady breath. When Matthew Blanchard wasn't being pompous, he was downright provocative. "I think I peppered the meatballs too much," she said, trying vainly to smile naturally at him.

He continued looking at her with a grave expression that reminded her of Lucy. "I realize this is tough on you," he said, "but I want you to know that I really appreciate you helping Lucy and me out like this."

She shrugged. "I wasn't doing anything, anyway."

"I know. Elaine told me . . . about your wrecked plans for the holidays. I'm sorry. This is not a good time of the year to be unhappy."

Something twisted inside Sherrie's stomach. So that was it. He was feeling sorry for her. Wondering exactly what Elaine had told him, she said offhandedly, "I wasn't as hurt as I might have been. I realize now that it wouldn't have worked anyway. My . . . Jason and I didn't really have that much in common. I think we were both lonely. We turned to each other for the wrong reasons."

Matt nodded. "I know how easily that can happen. And I know what a bad mistake that can be."

She wondered what he was trying to tell her. Had he realized she'd tried to get him and Elaine together, and wanted her to know he wasn't interested? Or worse, was he warning her not to get any ideas about him herself?

Well, he needn't worry on that score, she thought, lifting her chin. She wasn't in the least bit anxious to get involved with any man again, even if she did find him physically attractive... even sexy, if she were to be honest with herself.

Besides, the plan was to find him a wife. And she'd be the last person on earth Matthew Blanchard would consider for that role. He'd made that clear enough.

"Well..." She looked pointedly at the clock. "I'd better get up to Lucy's room before she falls asleep."

"You know where it is?"

"Yes, she showed me all her toys the minute we got to the house."

Matt smiled ruefully. "She has a lot of energy for a little girl. If it's any consolation, I can't remember ever seeing her this excited about Christmas. I imagine you had something to do with that."

"I guess she's looking forward to her Christmas wishes coming true," Sherrie said awkwardly, wondering what he'd say if he knew exactly what she'd promised his daughter.

"I hope you didn't promise her a horse," Matt said, looking uneasy. "That's one of her favorite wishes."

Sherrie managed a light laugh. "No, nothing like that." Actually Lucy's wish was going to be a lot tougher than a horse, she thought, but she wasn't about to tell him that.

"Well, that's a relief." Matt glanced down at his watch. "Lucy and I usually get up around seven. She has to be at kindergarten by nine."

Her heart skipped as she envisioned him coming down to breakfast wearing nothing but a robe, his hair tousled and morning stubble covering his jaw.

Annoyed with her lack of control over her unruly imagination, she said a quick good-night and left before her face could give her lecherous thoughts away.

She had better find a mother for Lucy soon, she told herself as she hurried up the stairs. She was becoming a little too preoccupied with the intimate aspects of her employer.

If ever there was a man totally unsuitable for Sherrie Latimer, it was Matthew Blanchard. They had absolutely nothing in common, and he was way out of her league. She wouldn't be comfortable with his life-style at all.

She smiled ruefully as she wondered what he would think if he could see the cluttered apartment she'd lived in until recently. He'd probably throw up his hands in horror. To her it was disorganized comfort. Compared to Matt's home, it was a mess.

He'd dump her just as quickly as he'd dumped his last wife, she assured herself as she walked into Lucy's room to check on the girl. And she would do well to remember that if she didn't want another broken heart.

Normally Matt liked to watch the late-evening news before going to bed. He found it kept his mind off his own problems, and he could fall asleep more easily. Tonight, however, he couldn't seem to concentrate on the dire predicament of the world.

The sports report seemed to make no sense, for once, and he missed the latest weather news. When he found himself switching channels in a vain attempt to find something interesting to watch, he turned the set off in disgust.

He was strangely reluctant to go to bed. His body was tired, but his mind kept reliving the events of the day the way a familiar song sometimes repeated itself over and over in his head. It was driving him crazy.

Maybe it was the thought of a strange woman sleeping in his house that made him so restless. No, he admitted reluctantly, it was the woman herself who was upsetting him.

He didn't know what to make of her. She confused and rattled him until he didn't know whether he was amused or irritated by her.

One thing he did know: she excited him in a way no woman ever had before. He hadn't relaxed since he'd arrived home from the store. He found himself constantly on guard, trying to keep his unpredictable emotions under control.

If it hadn't been such a dire emergency he'd have told her he'd changed his mind. He didn't need all this distraction. After all, Sherrie Latimer was not what he would call an accomplished housekeeper.

She appeared to be totally disorganized, and her cooking abilities were in some doubt, if he could judge from her attempt that evening. He'd nearly choked on the spicy meatballs. The only one who'd seemed to enjoy the meal was Lucy, and her taste buds weren't fully developed yet.

Matt leaned back in his easy chair and closed his eyes. She was good with Lucy, he'd give her that. And she was trying. After all, she was more or less doing him a favor. Given the choices, she was better than nothing.

He wondered what kind of jerk could have left her waiting in the church, all dressed up in her wedding gown, while he sent his best man to give her the bad news. The guy should be shot at dawn. No one deserved that. Especially an attractive, warmhearted, giving person like Sherrie.

Matt snapped his eyes open again. Now that thought was dangerous. That kind of thinking could get him in big trouble.

It had been bad enough avoiding the blatant moves of Elaine Maitland that evening. If she hadn't been a personal friend of Sherrie's, he would have ignored the woman altogether.

Women like Elaine were fairly easy to ignore. Someone like Sherrie on the other hand, with her innocent directness and subtle femininity, could creep up on a man, and he wouldn't know what had hit him until it was too late.

Matt sat up and carefully folded the newspaper. He wasn't about to let that happen again. He'd been soured by his experience, and he was damned if he was going to make another mistake.

He wasn't about to risk his daughter's happiness and peace of mind. She'd been too young to understand what was happening when her mother had left. She hadn't had to experience the kind of anger, pain and loss of self-esteem that he'd suffered.

But now Lucy was growing up. Next year she'd be in grade school. He wasn't going to let some woman steal his daughter's heart and then break it. Or his heart either for that matter. No, he and Lucy would do just fine as they were. Even if his conscience did prick him every year at Christmastime.

If it wasn't for the darn holiday season, he thought as he got wearily to his feet, he wouldn't have any doubts about his ability to give Lucy what she needed. It was seeing all those mothers visiting the toy department with their wide-eyed children. The guilt seemed to wrap itself around him like a thick, dark blanket. This was the time of year when a little girl needed a mother.

Four Christmas seasons he'd struggled through, trying not to blame himself for depriving his daughter of a true home and family...watching her watching the other kids with their mommies, her wistful expression tearing at his heart.

These were the times when he was uncomfortably aware that Lucy needed the special care and attention at home that a housekeeper, even an angel like Mrs. Halloway, couldn't give her.

But it wasn't enough to make him contemplate marriage again. Once Christmas was over, Matt told himself as he climbed the stairs, these feelings of guilt would go away, as they usually did.

Then he could concentrate on the New Year, and feel secure once more in the knowledge that he was doing his very best for his small daughter. Until then, he would have to grapple with the holidays the best way he knew how, and ignore all the sentimental, emotional hang-ups the season always brought with it.

And that, he thought emphatically, included the irrepressible Sherrie Latimer.

Sherrie awoke with a start, her heartbeat quickening as she looked up at the unfamiliar ceiling. She couldn't remember where she was for one thing, and for another, something cold and clammy was touching her face.

Turning her head, she came nose to nose with a massive, furry monster with glassy black eyes. She sat up with a shriek, and was answered by the high-pitched giggling of a child.

Memory flooded back at the sound. Sherrie peered around the head of the biggest stuffed beagle she'd ever seen, and gave Lucy a stern look. "What are you doing out of bed?"

"I brought Snoopy to surprise you," Lucy said, hugging the huge animal.

"Well, it worked." Sherrie eyed Snoopy's cold, black leather nose with respect. "But I think you could have waited until it was time to get up."

"It's almost eight o'clock." Lucy pointed to the bedside clock. "Daddy said to wake you up."

Sherrie looked at the clock with a gasp of dismay. She'd set the alarm, but obviously hadn't managed to set the unfamiliar clock correctly. "Oh, Lord," she muttered, thrusting back the covers. She had an hour to get Lucy washed, dressed, fed and in kindergarten. She didn't even know where kindergarten was.

Throwing open her suitcase, she scrambled through her things to find the silky black robe she'd bought for her honeymoon. She wished now that she'd brought something a little more serviceable. It had been an act of rebellion when she'd packed it yesterday.

She pulled it over the matching thigh-length nightgown and wrapped the satin cord around her waist. "Come on, sweetheart," she said, holding out her hand, "let's see how fast we can get ready for school."

Wondering where Matt was, she hoped he'd left already for the store. She was unprepared when he suddenly stepped out of his bedroom door in front of her.

He seemed just as startled as she was, his gaze sweeping intimately over her as if he couldn't quite believe what he was seeing.

"Hi, Daddy! I have to go to the bathroom," Lucy announced. She thrust Snoopy into Sherrie's arms, then ran past her father and closed the bedroom door behind her.

Matt acted as if he hadn't heard her. His face was turning a dull red and he didn't seem to know where to direct his gaze.

If Sherrie had been stark naked, she couldn't have felt more exposed. Conscious of her bare legs, she lowered Snoopy an inch or two to cover them.

She couldn't remember if she'd closed the neck of her robe, or left it gaping open. Not wanting to draw attention by looking, she raised Snoopy up again.

Her mouth felt suddenly dry, and she ran the tip of her tongue over her lips. "Good morning!" she croaked, trying vainly to sound unconcerned.

"You overslept..." Matt said, looking determinedly at a spot on the wall above her head. His voice sounded odd, too, as if he'd just stepped on a thumbtack with his bare foot.

"I know. Sorry about that. I did set the clock but it didn't work."

"I'll have a look at it later."

"Thanks, I'd appreciate that."

Matt cleared his throat. "I'll let you get dressed...er...get Lucy dressed, or she'll be late for kindergarten."

"We were on our way to the bathroom," Sherrie assured him unnecessarily. She took a tiny step toward him. Immediately he flattened himself against the wall, leaving enough room for an armored tank to pass.

She edged past him, just as Lucy opened the bathroom door again. "Daddy, are you coming to school with us?" she asked.

"Sorry, honey, I have to run," Matt said. "I'm late as well, now."

Pausing in the doorway, Sherrie wondered if he was blaming her for that. She watched him bend down and plant a firm kiss on Lucy's cheek. "I'll see you tonight, honey," he said, giving her narrow shoulders a squeeze.

"Kiss Snoopy, too." Lucy grabbed the dog from Sherrie and held it up to him.

Matt obediently touched his lips to Snoopy's nose.

A tiny shiver ran down Sherrie's back. Just a few moments ago her lips had touched the same spot.

"Now kiss Sherrie," Lucy demanded.

Matt jerked upright as if someone had tugged on his strings.

Sherrie's heart seemed to turn right over. "Come on, Lucy," she said quickly, and tugged on the little girl's hand to draw her into the bathroom. Before she closed the door, however, she caught a glimpse of Matt's face. He was standing quite still, looking as if he'd just lost his sense of direction.

"I'll see you at the store," she said quickly, and shut the door.

She was all fingers and thumbs. Twice she dropped the soap on the floor, and then she squeezed the toothpaste too hard, sending a thick, blue ribbon of paste across the counter. Lucy thought it was all a game, and shrieked with laughter, but Sherrie was inwardly cursing herself.

She couldn't let him do this to her. Hadn't she learned a hard enough lesson already? Surely she knew better than to let a man she hardly knew turn her world upside down? Especially a man who wasn't in the least bit interested in her—a man who was completely and totally opposite to her in every way. What was she thinking about?

It was the rebound, just as Elaine had pointed out, Sherrie warned herself as she pulled a green dress with purple trim over Lucy's head. Dragging a pair of white tights over the child's slender legs, she decided that she had to be sensible about this.

She'd been rejected, and was subconsciously looking for reassurance from another man. The fact that Matthew Blanchard was totally unsuitable was a good indication of the fact. He was off-limits, and so she felt safe in indulging in a little fantasizing.

At least, Sherrie reminded herself grimly, it would be safe as long as he didn't find out. She couldn't face the embarrassment if he ever got the slightest indication of the effect he had on her.

Operation Motherhood was becoming imperative, she thought as she poured cereal into a bowl for Lucy. Leaving the child to eat her breakfast with the television for company, Sherrie fled back upstairs and took a quick shower.

After dressing hurriedly in a long white sweater and black stretch pants, she rushed downstairs again. Her hair still felt damp and she hoped that wasn't going to mean a bad hair day. Not that it mattered that much, since her hair was hidden under a wig for the best part of the day.

It was ten minutes to nine when she coaxed Lucy into her green coat and wool hat, and found a pair of warm gloves for her. Finally seated in the car, Sherrie switched on the engine. Then she shut it off again. She'd forgotten to ask Matt for directions to the kindergarten.

Reluctant to leave Lucy in the car by herself, she waited patiently for the little girl to climb out, then hurried with her back into the house.

It took her a minute or two to look up the number of Blanchard's Department Store, then when she finally did get through, the operator put her on hold for what seemed like an eternity.

She watched the clock hand move toward the hour as she waited, her stomach tying up in knots, until the operator spoke in her ear.

"I'm sorry, Mr. Blanchard is not in his office."

"Can't you page him?" Sherrie asked. "This is his housekeeper. It's an emergency."

After another long frustrating wait, the operator came back on the line. "I"m sorry, ma'am, but we can't find him. He must not have arrived yet."

Where was he? Sherrie thought irritably. He'd left almost an hour ago. "You don't happen to know where his daughter goes to kindergarten, do you?" she asked desperately.

"I'm sorry, I don't," said the operator, beginning to sound worried. "I could try to find out for you."

"No, thanks," Sherrie said, glancing at the clock again. "That'll take too long. I'll manage. Thanks." She slammed down the receiver and headed back to the car with Lucy.

Starting the engine again, she said without much hope, "Lucy, sweetheart, do you think you could show me how to get to school?"

"I think so," Lucy said doubtfully.

Feeling a little more optimistic, Sherrie pulled out of the driveway. "Can you remember the name of it?"

"Uh-huh." Lucy thought for a moment. "I think it's called Peewee School," she said at last.

"Can you remember what street it's on?"

Lucy pointed straight ahead. "It's down there."

Half an hour later, Sherrie was forced to give up. Lucy had led her up and down the same street three times, but there was no sign of a building with the name of Peewee on it. Neither was there a kindergarten listed in the telephone book by that name.

There was nothing else she could do, Sherrie thought dismally, she would have to go back to the store and tell Matt what had happened. Her shift as Mrs. Claus was due to begin at ten, which was eleven minutes away. She'd barely have time to get into her costume as it was.

Matt had to be there by now. He would have to find someone else to take his daughter to kindergarten, if he wanted Mrs. Claus in her seat on time.

The store was already crowded with shoppers when Sherrie arrived there with Lucy. The little girl gasped for breath after the mad dash from the parking lot. Threading her way through the customers crowded around the fragrance counter, Sherrie caught sight of Beryl near the elevators. To her surprise, the woman hurried toward her with a frantic look on her face.

"Thank God," she said, reaching Sherrie's side. "Matt's going crazy up there." She peered down into Lucy's face. "Is she all right?"

"Of course she is. Except for the fact she's late for school." Sherrie felt a growing sense of uneasiness. "Is something wrong?"

Beryl shook her head, looking puzzled. "We thought there was. Matt got a message from Julie that there was some kind of emergency with Lucy. I think he's called every hospital, clinic and doctor within fifty miles of here."

It was Sherrie's turn to look puzzled. "Julie?"

"The operator who took the message from you. She said you were looking for Lucy. When I left Matt five minutes ago he was calling the police."

# Chapter Six

Sherrie's stomach felt as if she'd just plunged out of a plane. "Oh, Lord," she muttered. "Now I've done it."

"You'd better get up there and put him out of his misery," Beryl said, her look of sympathy only making Sherrie feel worse.

She gulped as she prodded the button on the elevator. She was probably going to lose both jobs, she thought as the door slid open.

"Good luck!" Beryl called out as she hurried away. Sherrie wished she could go with her.

Lucy tugged her hand as the door closed and the elevator soared to the sixth floor. "Is Daddy mad at us?" she asked.

Sherrie gave her a tense smile. "No, honey, he's not mad at you." He was likely to throw Mrs. Claus out the sixth-floor window, though, she added silently. Thinking furiously, she went over her conversation with the operator. It was hard to remember everything she said. Obviously she'd given Julie the wrong impression.

Stepping out into the hallway, Sherrie saw Matt's door standing open. Lucy broke free and ran for the office, while Sherrie followed more slowly.

She heard Matt's exclamation as Lucy ran into the office. When Sherrie reached the door she saw him standing by his desk, with Lucy held tight in his arms and his chin buried in his child's blond curls.

Sherrie stood awkwardly in the doorway, until Lucy wriggled to get down. "Me and Sherrie went for a long ride," she said as Matt turned slowly toward the door.

"Hi," Sherrie said lamely, wincing when she saw the strain on his face.

"What happened?" he said hoarsely.

"I...we...got lost...kind of."

Matt stared at her for a long, tense moment. "You got *lost?*" he said at last, his voice rising on the last word.

Sherrie nodded miserably. "I forgot to ask you where Lucy went to kindergarten and I called the store but you weren't here and I didn't want her to be late and she said she knew where it was and we were driving up and down..."

Matt moved to his chair and sank down. Reaching for the phone, he dialed a number, then said in a terse, crisp voice, "This is Matthew Blanchard. Please tell Officer Brooks that my daughter is safe and sound. Apparently there was a mistake in communications. Please tell him I am sorry to have bothered him." He paused, then added dryly into the phone, "And wish all of you a Merry Christmas." He put the receiver down again and leaned his head in his hands.

Sherrie looked back at him helplessly. "I'm sorry," she said. "I asked the operator if she knew where Lucy went to school. She must have misunderstood."

Matt nodded. "I called the kindergarten. When they said she hadn't arrived, I thought—" He broke off and reached for his daughter to give her another tight hug.

"It wasn't Sherrie's fault," Lucy said in a small voice. "I couldn't find the school."

"It's all right, honey." Matt dropped a kiss on his daughter's head. "I'll take you to school. Sherrie has work to do."

Her heart lifted when she realized she still had the Mrs. Claus job, at least. "I'll get there as soon as possible," she said, and escaped from the room.

At least she hadn't let Tom down, she thought as she scrambled into her costume. But Matt was probably never going to trust her with his daughter again. And she couldn't blame him one bit. Of course, that didn't make it hurt any less.

She realized now how fond she was becoming of Lucy. She would miss her a great deal, she thought as she made her way down to the Christmas display. Maybe it would be for the best to lose her job as Matt's housekeeper. If she stayed around the Blanchards much longer, she would find it very hard to leave the little girl.

She refused to listen to the tiny voice in her mind, which added that it would be just as hard to leave Matt. He certainly wouldn't miss her, she thought ruefully. The expression on his face when he'd seen her standing in the doorway told her exactly what he was thinking.

She just wasn't responsible enough to take care of his daughter. That was the bottom line. In fact, it seemed that she messed up everything she did lately. Apparently she just wasn't cut out to be a wife and mother, so she was thankful now that her marriage with Jason hadn't gone through. It was better to have found out now, than to wait until she had a baby to discover she wasn't capable of taking care of it.

Feeling immensely sorry for herself, she took her seat on the red velvet chair. The line of eager children buzzed with excitement as she beckoned to the first child.

It wasn't long before she forgot her own troubles. Child after child climbed up onto her lap, making her smile with their eager questions, sometimes surprising her with their sharp minds, and more than once bringing a tear to her eye with their simple requests.

Absorbed in their whimsical wants and needs, the time flew by, until shortly before Sherrie was due to quit for the day, she looked up and saw Lucy standing in front of her.

Knowing Matt wouldn't be far away, Sherrie glanced over at the toy department. Matt stood in his usual spot, watching the activities of the children among the crammed shelves.

Her heart seemed to flip over when she saw his face. He reminded her of a child with his face pressed up to a window, looking in at some longed-for treasure he knew he could never have.

Following his gaze, Sherrie saw a woman with a little girl about Lucy's age. She was pointing to the various dolls on the shelf, apparently pointing out the best features of each one. More than likely she was finding out which one her daughter preferred before buying her one for Christmas.

It was during the holidays when people missed their loved ones the most, Sherrie thought with a pang. Was Matt missing his ex-wife, thinking about what he had lost? Was he still in love with her? The ache in her heart deepened at the thought.

"Hi, Mrs. Claus," said a tiny voice.

Forgetting Matt for the moment, Sherrie smiled as Lucy climbed into her lap. "Hi, Lucy," she said, making an effort to disguise her voice. "Did you have a good time at school today?"

Lucy nodded. "I was late, but Daddy 'splained to the teacher and she said it was okay." She spread out the fingers of both hands. "I'm learning to count up to twenty," she said proudly.

"You are? Can you count for me?" Out of the corner of her eye Sherrie saw Matt glance their way, then look back at the toy shelves. Probably checking up on her to make sure she didn't lose his daughter, Sherrie thought, and was immediately ashamed of her pettiness. Lucy was all Matt had. Of course he was protective of her. If she were Lucy's mother she'd be the same way.

The way things were going, she thought miserably, it was unlikely she'd ever have children of her own. The poignant thought seemed to pierce her heart.

Lucy was counting slowly and laboriously. Finally she announced a triumphant, "Twenty!"

Sherrie gave her a big hug. "That was wonderful, sweetheart. You did a great job."

"Did you find a mommy yet?" Lucy asked, her eyes suddenly intent on Sherrie's face. The expression was so much like her father's that Sherrie caught her breath.

"Not yet, honey." She glanced back at Matt, but he was looking somewhere else. "Finding a mommy is a very tough thing to do."

"But you can do it, 'cos you're Mrs. Claus and she can do everything." Lucy spread out her arms to emphasize her point.

"I think you're getting me mixed up with *Mr.* Claus," Sherrie said wryly.

"Well, can't you ask him to find me and Daddy a mommy?"

Sherrie sighed. If only it were that simple. "I'll keep on trying," she said, "but you mustn't mind too much if I don't find one before Christmas. It might take me a little longer than that."

"But you'll be gone after Christmas," Lucy said, looking as if she were about to cry. "And so will Sherrie."

Sherrie's heart gave an uncomfortable jump. She'd be gone a lot sooner than that, she thought, worriedly. How would Lucy feel about that?

"Well, you did know that Sherrie wouldn't be able to stay for very long," she said gently.

"Why not?" Lucy looked up at her. "Why can't Sherrie be my new mommy?"

Oh, Lord, Sherrie thought. She should have anticipated this. "Because Sherrie isn't a mommy person," she said, a little helplessly.

Lucy looked puzzled. "Why not? I think she's a mommy person."

"I'm sorry, sweetheart, but some people are better at being mommies than others." Sherrie looked desperately over at Matt. "I think your daddy's looking for you, so you'd better run along. I'll see you tomorrow, Lucy."

Lucy's accusing gaze cut right through her heart. "You said you would find me a mommy," she said, her lower lip trembling.

"I'll try, sweetheart, that's all I can do. I promise I will do my very best."

How she hated the feeling that she had let the child down, Sherrie thought as she watched Lucy trudge over to her father. She should never have even hinted that she might be able to pull off what amounted to a miracle.

Miracles happened sometimes, she knew, especially at Christmastime, but not to people like her or Lucy. They just weren't needy enough. There were too many people out there with far worse problems looking for miracles.

Though if only the powers-that-be who granted such marvels could look into that child's eyes when she talked about finding a new mommy, Sherrie thought as she eased up out of the chair, there would be no doubt about Lucy's powerful need.

She hung up her sign announcing that Mrs. Claus had gone back to the North Pole for the night, then stepped off the platform. Her heart skipped a beat when she saw Matt standing by the elevators.

He still had Lucy by the hand, and she felt a flutter of panic. She hoped he wouldn't fire her in front of his daughter. In any case, she thought worriedly, as she watched him disappear with Lucy into the elevator, she would have to go back to the house to pick up her belongings. How was she going to explain to Lucy that she'd messed up and had to leave?

She waited until she was sure Matt would be back in his office before heading for the elevators. Once she reached the employees' lounge she hurried into her street clothes, taking care to hang up her costume before running a comb through her tangled hair.

The thought of going back to Tom's lonely apartment depressed her. She would have to buy some decorations, she decided, and a Christmas tree. That would help cheer up the place.

Catching sight of her miserable face in the mirror, she frowned. She should be ashamed of herself, she silently told her reflection. There were thousands, perhaps millions of people in the world without food and shelter for Christmas. She had both. She should be thinking about the less fortunate, instead of worrying about her own petty little problems.

Slowly she lowered the comb, as an idea sprang to her mind, lifting her spirits. She could do what Tom was doing—use her spare time to help out the less fortunate. It would certainly help to pass the time, and she might be able to help perform some of those minor miracles. It might help to make up for letting Lucy down.

Reaching for her jacket, Sherrie considered the possibilities. Her next-door neighbor at her old apartment could help her find somewhere where she was needed. Maria Benitto was always volunteering for some charity or other. Ever since her husband had died she'd had too much time on her hands, she'd told Sherrie one day. Her volunteer work kept her from brooding about feeling lonely.

If it worked for Maria, then it could work for her, Sherrie thought as she walked slowly down the hallway to Matt's office. It would certainly be better than moping around Tom's apartment on her own.

She could hear Lucy's high-pitched voice when she tapped on the door of Matt's office. Answering his summons, she opened the door and walked in. She avoided looking at Matt, who was seated behind his desk, as usual. Lucy sat on the edge of a swivel chair, twisting it from side to side. She looked up with a smile as Sherrie approached the desk.

"Hi, Sherrie! Guess what! I can count to twenty." She spread out her fingers and counted each one while Sherrie watched, a hard lump growing in her throat.

"That's wonderful, sweetheart," she whispered when Lucy reached the last finger. "I'm very proud of you." She blinked hard as Lucy beamed up at her.

"I wonder if you could stop off on the way home and pick up some dry cleaning for me," Matt said, his voice sounding gruff.

Sherrie noticed that one of Lucy's shoelaces was untied. She leaned down to tie it up again, saying a little breathlessly, "Sure. Which cleaners do you use?"

She was relieved when Matt gave her the name of one she knew. He was probably waiting until he got home before firing her, she decided. At least then he wouldn't have to do it in front of Lucy. Though she could hardly leave without saying goodbye to the little girl. Lucy would probably cry.

Sherrie hoped she'd be able to get out of there without breaking down into tears herself. She'd be seeing Lucy at the store, of course, but she couldn't tell her that. And those few moments she had with the little girl as Mrs. Claus would be painfully brief.

Even now, at the thought of having to turn her back on Matt's daughter, she could feel tears prickling her eyelids. She had done what she had tried her utmost not to do: she had given her heart to the child. And now it was about to be broken.

Aware that Matt had asked her a question, Sherrie finished tying Lucy's shoelace and straightened up. "Sorry, what did you say?"

"I asked if you knew how to find the cleaners."

Flushing, she lifted her chin. "I know where it is. I promise not to get lost again."

To her surprise, he actually smiled. Handing her a square, white ticket, he said, "I'm going to be home a little later tonight, so you might want to hold dinner until I get there."

For a moment she could only stare at him. Then she said warily, "You want me to cook dinner?"

Matt's eyebrows rose. "I thought that's what I hired you to do."

Heady with relief, she looked down at Lucy, then back at Matt's confused face. "I thought—" She broke off as she saw disbelief on his face.

"You thought I was going to fire you?"

Sherrie shrugged. "After the mess up this morning, I thought you might decide I wasn't fit to take care of your daughter." Matt stared at her, and she could feel herself growing warm as she wondered what was going through his mind.

Even Lucy seemed intimidated by her father's lengthy silence. She sat with her feet slowly swinging back and forth while she watched his face.

Finally Matt said quietly, "You can rest assured I have no intention of firing you. I have no one else to take care of Lucy."

Well, that certainly cleared things up. Sherrie made an effort to relax her shoulders. He had no choice but to keep her on. After all, if he'd been able to find a real housekeeper, he wouldn't have hired her in the first place. That was why she'd been given this reprieve. The man was desperate.

Nevertheless, she couldn't stop the sudden leap of her spirits as she held out her hand to Lucy. She wouldn't have to go back to Tom's dreary apartment after all. "Come on, sweetheart," she said softly, "let's go home."

"Why did you think Daddy wanted to burn you?" Lucy asked, as she sat next to Sherrie in the car a few minutes later.

"Burn me?" For a moment, Sherrie was puzzled. Then she laughed. "Not burn, sweetheart. Fire me. It means to let me go." That didn't sound right, either, she realized. She tried again. "When you fire someone it means that you don't want them to work for you anymore."

Lucy digested this in silence. Then she said in a small voice, "I don't want to fire you. I like you being our housekeeper. I hope Mrs. Halloway never comes back."

Sherrie glanced at Lucy's unhappy face and felt a pang of apprehension. The little girl would take it hard when the time came for Sherrie to leave.

It might have been better if Matt had fired her that afternoon, after all. The more time she spent with Lucy, the more attached the child would become.

On the other hand, now that she was still the Blanchards' housekeeper, she could concentrate on her search for a mother once more. Once Lucy had another woman in her life, it would make the parting with Sherrie easier. Sooner or later, Lucy would forget all about her, Sherrie thought, with a bittersweet pang of regret.

With one ear on Lucy's chatter, she thought about the kind of woman she needed to find. Someone mature, and a homebody. Someone who was expert at taking care of of others. Someone like her ex-neighbor, Maria Benitto, for instance, who used her spare time to help others.

In fact, Sherrie thought, with a spark of excitement, why not Maria Benitto? She would be perfect. Maria might be three or four years older than Matt, but with her dark hair and flashing black eyes, she was still an attractive woman. Having raised four children of her own, she would certainly know what she was doing as far as Lucy was concerned, and Matt would have a mature, intelligent companion.

Not only that, Sherrie thought, warming to her idea, Maria was a superb cook. She was a sous-chef at an Italian restaurant, and Sherrie had sampled a couple of her favorite dishes.

Most important of all, Maria was lonely and was looking for love and companionship. Perhaps she would find what she was looking for with the Blanchards.

Stifling her pangs of envy, Sherrie decided to set things up as soon as possible. Somehow she had to find an excuse for Maria to visit the house, and then invite her to stay for the evening. And this time, she decided, she would arrange it so that Matt and Maria were alone. She didn't want to watch them getting to know each other. She'd rather not be there when Matt realized what a wonderful wife and mother Maria would make.

Matt sat for a long time at his desk after Sherrie had left with Lucy. He'd had no idea until now that Sherrie's self-esteem was so low. She'd really expected him to fire her after this morning's mix-up.

Matt sighed, and leaned back in his chair. True, he might have been more reassuring when she'd finally turned up with Lucy, but he'd been out of his mind with worry. He was afraid that in his relief at seeing his daughter alive and well, he might have lost control and done something stupid.

He sat forward again and ran his fingers through his hair. Much as he hated to admit it, when he'd seen Sherrie standing in the doorway looking so worried, he'd felt a tremendous urge to rush over there and kiss away that look of misery on her face.

He'd realized, of course, what a mistake that would be. Just remembering that fleeting impulse set warning bells clamoring in his head.

To make matters worse, he'd almost given in to the urge again when she'd told him she didn't think she was fit to take care of his daughter. Maybe it was that look of desperate vulnerability, or perhaps the defiant little lift of her chin that he found so endearing. Whatever it was, he'd been reminded forcefully of just how long it had been since he'd held a woman in his arms.

"Damn." Matt picked up a pencil and threw it at the window. Maybe he *should* have fired her. She was a danger to his well-controlled world. It had taken him years to feel secure with the way his life was going. He had it all mapped out now, and it was simple.

He would continue to run the store until after Lucy was through with college, and had happily settled down with a family of her own. Then he'd be free to do some traveling, maybe buy a motor home and see more of the vast, diverse country he lived in.

He wanted nothing to disrupt that clear and uncomplicated path. It had taken him too long to come to terms with the future as he saw it. Once he had set his course, he was determined to stay on it, come what may. That was Matthew Blanchard's way.

He didn't know why he saw Sherrie Latimer as a threat to his objective. He only knew that from the first moment he'd seen her standing in front of his desk with those ridiculous wisps of cotton sticking to her face, his carefully constructed world had been shaken. And that worried him a great deal.

Deciding he needed a change of scenery, he left the office and headed for the elevator. Maybe if he mingled with the customers, he told himself as he descended rapidly to the main floor, he'd get a better perspective of what was going on in his head.

It was the Christmas season, of course, that was messing up his mind. Every year there was something. Last year it was the horse that Lucy had begged him to buy. She could have had anything in the entire store, but she had to have a real, live horse.

It was out of the question, of course. Not only was it impractical, but Lucy was too young to be trusted on the back of a horse. It was a whim that would quickly pass. He'd known that, and in fact, Lucy had forgotten about it long before her February birthday.

But right up until Christmas Eve he'd fought with his common sense, and had very nearly rushed out at the last minute and bought the damn horse.

Stepping out of the elevator, Matt assured himself that it would be the same this year. In a couple of weeks or so Christmas would be over, Mrs. Halloway would be back and he could forget that Sherrie Latimer ever existed. He deliberately ignored the little voice in his head that wryly whispered, *Good luck.*

Without a doubt, Sherrie thought, frowning at the contents of the freezer, cooking dinner presented her biggest problem. She was used to taking out a frozen entrée and throwing it into the microwave. She'd add maybe a few frozen vegetables, or more likely a salad, and enjoy a simple, but well-balanced meal.

Somehow, after viewing the packages of chicken, beef and various other unidentified objects, Sherrie got the impression that Mrs. Halloway would shudder at the thought of frozen fish sticks. Though she did keep a packet or two of vegetables in the freezer, Sherrie was relieved to see.

Browsing through a thick cookbook, she found a simple-looking recipe for a champagne chicken dinner. An anxious hunt through the cabinets turned up the rest of the ingredients. She even found a bottle of champagne hidden in the back of the fridge. Even Lucy would enjoy the dish, once the alcohol was cooked out of the champagne.

She was anxiously watching a package of chicken thaw in the microwave when she heard the front door slam. Her heart skipped crazily as she heard Lucy call a greeting to her father, followed by Matt's deep-voiced response.

She waited, heart pounding, for him to come into the kitchen, but after several anxious minutes had passed she realized he must have joined Lucy in the living room in front of the television.

Intensely disappointed, she began furiously chopping up a bunch of green onions. She had just finished measuring them when the door opened without warning and Matt peered around it.

His pleasant expression changed to one of concern when he saw her. "What's the matter?" he asked sharply.

She dashed a hand across her eyes as he came into the kitchen. "Nothing," she said nasally. "I've been chopping onions, that's all."

"Oh." He looked relieved, and shoved his hands into his slacks pockets. "What are you cooking?"

"Champagne chicken." She lifted the lid off the small red potatoes, which were bubbling merrily in the saucepan.

"Well," Matt said lightly, "that sounds almost as good as spaghetti and meatballs."

Sensing the hint of sarcasm, Sherrie winced. "I'm measuring everything," she said, her voice stiff with resentment. "So there shouldn't be any mistakes." She kept her gaze on the stove as she replaced the lid.

After a short pause, Matt said awkwardly, "Well, I'd better keep out of your way. I'll help Lucy set the table." He gathered up a fistful of silverware from the drawer and hurried out of the kitchen as if he were glad of the excuse to leave.

Sherrie sighed. He would never see her as anything but an awkward, irresponsible adolescent. And he was right. It was the story of her life. No matter how hard she tried, somehow she always messed up. She was a confirmed klutz, and she was stuck with it.

She wouldn't mind so much, she thought mournfully, if it wasn't for Matt. She cared what he thought of her. Maybe she cared a little too much. Maybe she should worry about that.

# Chapter Seven

Peering at the recipe, Sherrie tried to concentrate on the directions. The potatoes were almost ready, the frozen peas and pearl onions would only take about four minutes. It was time to tackle the difficult part.

Sherrie carefully laid the pieces of boneless chicken breast in the hot butter and left them to brown. She measured out the whipped cream, and then eyed the bottle of champagne. She'd never opened a bottle of champagne in her life.

She thought about asking Matt to do it, but decided against it. This was one dinner she was determined to make without any outside help.

After tearing the silver cap off the cork, she examined the wire holding it down. It didn't look too complicated. After all, she'd seen waiters do it all the time in movies.

She stuck the bottle between her knees and braced her thumbs against the wire. Taking a deep breath, she shoved upward. The loud pop made her jump. The bottle jerked in her hands, and champagne gushed out of the bottle, while the cork shot up to the ceiling and smacked back down again.

She didn't see where it landed, she was too busy staring at the puddle spreading in front of her feet.

The door suddenly swung open and Matt rushed in, his face creased in anxiety. "What the devil was that?" he demanded.

Sighing, Sherrie held up the bottle. "It came out faster than I expected," she said.

She was annoyed to see Matt's mouth twitch. "That's a pretty expensive way to wash the floor," he said mildly.

Sherrie jutted out her chin. Trust a man to make fun of an awkward situation. "I'm sorry," she said, determined not to let him unsettle her again. "This happens to be the first time I've opened a bottle of champagne. I guess I didn't handle it properly."

Matt nodded. His eyes still glimmered with amusement, but his expression remained grave. "I figured as much. Why didn't you ask me to do it?"

"I didn't want to bother you with it."

She flinched as he studied her face, but she refused to drop her gaze. "Besides," she added defiantly, "I wanted to do it myself."

"Very commendable," Matt murmured. "Just promise me that you'll ask for my help if you decide to tackle something really dangerous for the first time. Like changing a wheel on the car, for instance."

To her horror she felt tears of resentment beginning to well up beneath her lashes. "I might be incompetent," she said, trying desperately to stop her voice from quivering, "but at least I'm willing to try. That's better than giving up before the attempt."

Matt's amusement vanished at once. He moved toward her, concern in his face. "Hey," he said gently, "I'm sorry. I didn't mean to hurt your feelings. I admire you for being independent and wanting to do things for yourself. I've met too many women who pretend to be helpless just to get what they want. It's refreshing to meet someone who can take care of herself."

Totally disarmed by this sudden display of compassion, Sherrie's resentment vanished. "I'm not sure I do such a good job of looking after myself," she said ruefully. "Tom is always telling me what a klutz I am. He's constantly checking up on me. I think he's afraid if he doesn't keep an eye on me I'll do something really stupid and hurt myself."

Looking up at Matt's face at such close quarters was definitely unnerving, she decided as he studied her with a thoughtful frown. In fact, her knees were beginning to lock together for support. He had such a sensual mouth. She wanted so much to know how it would feel to be kissed by that mouth. She couldn't seem to stop thinking about it.

She backed away and put the bottle down on the kitchen table. "I'd better clean up that mess," she said hurriedly, "before Lucy comes in and walks it all over the kitchen." Grabbing hold of a mop, she began dabbing at the puddle on the floor.

"Your brother must care for you a great deal," Matt said quietly.

Startled by the comment, she shrugged. "I guess so. There are times, though, when I wish he didn't care quite so much. Ever since our parents died he's kind of felt responsible for me, I guess. He was the first one to warn me about Jason, and he was right."

She lifted the mop and carried it to the sink to squeeze it out. "That's the trouble," she said. "Tom is nearly always right. He's always been the sensible one, the organized one, the sane, quiet, composed one. I tend to jump into things without thinking. I follow my instincts instead of rationalizing everything the way Tom does. It gets me in trouble at times."

Matt was quiet while she finished mopping the floor. Then, as she put the mop away, he said gently, "It would be a very dull world if we were all the same, Sherrie. Don't be so hard on yourself. There's no rule that says you have to be like your brother. You are unique. Be happy with that."

She turned to look at him, caught off guard by this personal observation. His eyes no longer gleamed with amusement, or even compassion. She saw something else in the sky blue depths of his gaze—a sudden flaring of heat that set her pulse fluttering like the windblown ribbons of a high-flying kite.

Ripples of warmth surfed from her head to her toes, chased by chills of excitement. She wished she still had hold of the mop, because now she didn't know what to do with her hands.

She wanted to speak, to break the spell that seemed to hold her motionless, but all she could think about was the fascinating way his dark brows curved slightly above his hooded eyes.

His lips parted, allowing a quiet, shuddering breath to escape. At the soft sound, something deep inside her began to uncurl like the petals of a summer rose in the heat of midday. She couldn't breathe, couldn't move a muscle.

She was intensely aware of the strong slope of his shoulders beneath the striped shirt. She could see the faint rise and fall of his chest, and she wanted to lay her hand against his heartbeat. She wanted to feel the rasping stroke of his chin against her cheek. She wanted, in the worst way, to know the warm pressure of his mouth on hers. She waited in agonizing suspense for him to make a move, willing him to close the gap between them.

His gaze locked with hers. His voice rasped in his throat as he whispered, "Sherrie, I—" He broke off, lifting his head sharply. "Do I smell something burning?"

It took her a moment or two to realize what he'd said. Then, feeling as if she'd just stepped under a stream of ice-cold water, she snapped out of her daze. "Oh, Lord," she wailed. "My dinner!"

She dashed over to the stove, and dragged the smoking pan from the ring. Now that she was right on top of the frying pan, she could hardly stand the smell. Staring at the blackened chicken, she saw something that wasn't supposed to be there.

Peering closer at the foreign object, she finally recognized it. "I don't believe it," she muttered.

"Believe what?" Matt asked behind her.

Turning, she thrust the pan at him. "Look at that. Only my lousy luck could have achieved that."

Matt peered at the mess in the pan. "What is it?"

"It's the champagne cork. It must have hit the ceiling and bounced right down into my chicken." Her voice rose in anguish. "My dinner's ruined!"

Matt made an odd sound in his throat.

Sherrie glared at him, then slammed the pan down on the stove. "Don't you dare laugh," she said threateningly. "If you do you'll be wearing this mess in your hair."

"I was just going to suggest you pass it off as Cajun cooking," Matt said, in a choked voice. "I'm sorry, I can't seem to help—" He broke off with a strangled gasp.

Sherrie stared at him, infuriated. He was turning red in the face with the effort not to laugh. "If you knew the trouble I went to—" she started indignantly, but she was interrupted by a low rumble of laughter from Matt's throat.

It was the first time she'd heard him laugh. The sound was so infectious, her indignation vanished as quickly as it had arisen. She found herself smiling, then chuckling, until she was laughing out loud with him.

"I told you I was a klutz," she said, between gusts of laughter. "I'm dangerous to be around."

His laughter died so suddenly she was shocked into silence as well. Once more she saw the heat in his eyes, and this time there was a gleam of purpose behind it. It was as if something had snapped, tearing down whatever barrier had been between them before.

"You're dangerous to be around all right," he said thickly.

She trembled, sensing what was coming and now suddenly apprehensive. Her heart froze, then began thudding against her ribs as he took a step toward her.

For a second or two panic swept over her. This wasn't supposed to be happening. She was risking her heart once more, and she'd promised herself never to do that again.

Then he closed the distance between them and took a firm hold of her arms. The second he touched her, all her doubts were blown away like wisps of smoke in the wind. Eagerly she tilted her head back and closed her eyes as his mouth descended hard on hers.

It was a long, lingering kiss, firm and inquiring, and not in the least threatening. She raised her arms and clung to his broad shoulders, certain she had never felt so heady with excitement in her entire life.

He folded his arms around her as he deepened the kiss, and her insides seemed to melt. He smelled of cedar and fir, holly and mistletoe, and the exotic spices of the East.

The sweet, warm taste of his mouth on hers seemed to envelop her in a fuzzy glow, and she basked in it as she clung to him. Forgetting all her inhibitions, she kissed him back with all her heart and soul.

Then she felt his shoulder muscles tense beneath her fingers, and abruptly, it was over. Her warm glow faded as he let her go, and she grew cold when she saw the closed expression on his face.

"I'm sorry...I shouldn't have...er...Lucy will be wondering where I am...." He shook his head, as if trying to clear his mind, then he dragged open the door and disappeared.

Sherrie stood quite still as the silent seconds ticked by. She could still feel the imprint of his mouth, warm and tender on hers. She lifted her hand to touch her lips with the tips of her fingers. He had kissed her. He had actually kissed her. And the sensations she had felt had been beyond her wildest dreams.

She could feel the ache begin as she remembered the look on his face when he'd let her go. He'd apologized. He'd made a mistake and instantly regretted it. He'd made that clear enough.

With an effort she pulled herself together and reached for the frying pan. What else could she expect? He'd been carried away by the moment. It was Christmas, and things like that happened this time of the year. She should know that better than anyone.

It had been Christmas Eve when Jason had proposed. Unfortunately he'd waited a whole year before admitting he'd made a mistake.

Sherrie opened the lid of the trash bin and emptied the contents of the pan into it. She was quite certain that Matt wouldn't wait as long as Jason had. He'd make sure she knew that he regretted his rash action just as soon as the opportunity arose.

Well, she decided as she took out a fresh package of chicken from the freezer, she wasn't going to look like the fool. She would die before she let him know how much his kiss had affected her. She would just brush it off as if she hadn't given it a second thought. Then he wouldn't have to feel so guilty.

The door opened, making her jump. For a moment she thought it was Matt coming back to set her straight on his intentions. But then Lucy stuck her head around the door.

"Daddy says if you want to he'll take us out to dinner," she said, coming into the room.

Sherrie gave her a tired smile. "Tell Daddy thanks, but I want to make this dinner."

Lucy looked disappointed. "Okay, I'll tell him." She disappeared, and Sherrie made a face. It was nice of Matt to suggest going out after she'd messed up the dinner, but he could have at least come and told her himself.

Sighing, she stuck the chicken into the microwave to defrost. Now to give it a second shot, she thought as she checked out the rest of the ingredients.

Lucy came back into the kitchen a short while later. "Is dinner nearly ready?" she asked. "I'm hungry."

Sherrie wondered if Matt had sent her in to ask, then chided herself for her pettiness. Smiling at the little girl, she said brightly, "It's almost ready. About another five minutes. I bet your daddy's hungry, too."

Lucy shrugged. "I dunno. He won't talk to me. He sounds cross. He says he doesn't feel like talking and he wants to watch the TV."

"I expect he's just tired," Sherrie said, trying to ignore the ache in her heart. "He's been working really hard at the store."

"I know." Lucy sniffed the air. "It smells good."

"I hope it tastes good." Sherrie lifted the chicken out of the pan and put it into the oven to keep warm. She studied the directions one last time, then nervously made the sauce.

It looked all right, she thought, when it was done. She dipped an experimental finger into it then licked it. It actually tasted pretty good, though whether it would be up to Mrs. Halloway's standards, she had serious doubts.

A few minutes later she sat at the table anxiously waiting for Matt to taste the dinner. He had barely glanced at her when he'd taken his seat at the head of the table. She knew he was feeling awkward about what happened and didn't know quite how to deal with it.

She was having problems with the situation herself. She wasn't sure whether to pretend the kiss never happened, or acknowledge that it did and make light of it.

After cutting up Lucy's chicken for her, she filled her own plate, trying desperately not to watch Matt out of the corner of her eye.

Finally, to her intense relief, he said in a voice barely hiding his surprise, "This is very good."

"It's almost as good as the basketty," Lucy said, clinching the success of the meal.

Smiling back at the little girl, Sherrie said lightly, "Well, thank you one and all. I'm happy you're enjoying it. It's a new recipe I tried out."

"Daddy likes those little fishy things that swim around on your plate," Lucy announced.

Sherrie sent Matt an inquiring glance.

"Scampi," he explained.

Of course. She should have known.

"He likes basketty, too, don't you, Daddy?"

"I sure do, Lucy." He looked a little embarrassed. "Was there any champagne left?" he asked, laying down his fork.

"Yes, I'll get it."

She made to get up, but he stopped her with a lift of his hand. "I will. You finish your dinner."

Sherrie watched him leave the room, aware of the growing ache around her heart. She should never have let it get this far, she thought miserably.

They were actually beginning to relax with each other until this happened. Now they were back where they started, only now they had this awkward situation between them. It seemed unlikely they would ever be able to relax with each other again.

And that, Sherrie told herself with mounting dejection, would be the saddest thing of all.

Dinner was almost over when Matt said suddenly, "How would you like to go to a special Christmas show tomorrow, Lucy?"

The little girl dropped her fork, her eyes lighting up. "What kind of show?"

"It's an ice show, with lots of your favorite characters from the television show you like so much. You don't have to go to school the next day, so it won't hurt if you're late to bed."

"Oh, right!" Lucy said, bouncing up and down in her excitement. "Can Sherrie come, too?"

Matt looked embarrassed. "I'm sorry, Lucy, I could only get tickets for the two of us."

"Oh, that's all right," Sherrie said quickly. "I have plenty to do here."

"Friday is usually Mrs. Halloway's day off," Matt said, aiming his glance somewhere above her head. "I'm sure you can use the time."

She tried to hide her disappointment. "As a matter of fact," she said brightly, "I do have to look for a new apartment. I can do that tomorrow evening."

"Fine, then it's settled." Matt rose, his gaze still avoiding hers. "I'll catch up on the news until Lucy's ready for her bedtime story."

She watched him leave the room, wishing she didn't hurt so much inside. He had made it pretty obvious he regretted giving in to such a rash impulse. He was probably terrified she would read too much into it. No doubt she would receive a lecture before the night was out, warning her not to take him seriously.

Lucy slipped from her chair, and ran around the table. Slipping her hand into Sherrie's, she said forlornly, "I wish you could have come with us to the show."

Sherrie smiled, and ran her hand over the dark blond curls. "Well, sweetheart, I think it's good that a little girl should have her daddy all to herself now and again."

"It would be lots better if I had a mommy, too."

Feeling a catch in her throat, Sherrie got up quickly from her chair. "Okay, pardner," she drawled, in a bad imitation of John Wayne, "it's gettin' kinda late here. You've gotta have your bath now, little lady."

She took the little girl's hand and led her upstairs, then did her best to chase away Lucy's despondency by playing a boisterous game with her bath toys that resulted in a very wet bathroom floor.

After tucking her into bed later, Sherrie dropped a soft kiss on the small forehead. Lucy answered by wrapping her arms around her neck. "I'm really glad you're our housekeeper, Sherrie. I don't want Mrs. Halloway to ever come back. She's not fun like you are."

A surge of tenderness robbed Sherrie of her voice for a moment or two. She straightened, and took her time tucking in the covers, until she could speak naturally again. "You know," she said carefully, "this is really Mrs. Halloway's job. She takes very good care of you. Much better than I can. I'm just filling in for her while she's away. She'll be coming back after Christmas and I know you'll be happy to see her."

"No, I won't," Lucy said vigorously. "I don't want her to come back."

Her heart heavy, Sherrie looked down at the little girl. "I don't belong here, sweetheart. I have another job to go to, and I won't be able to stay after Christmas. If Mrs. Halloway doesn't come back, you won't have anyone to look after you and Daddy."

Obviously put out by this argument, Lucy jutted out her lower lip. "Yes, we will," she said, with such conviction Sherrie felt a pang of cold apprehension. "I'm going to have a new mommy, so there. Mrs. Claus promised me I would. So she can look after me and Daddy."

Sherrie did her best to smile at the little girl. "Sweetheart, Mrs. Claus can't always bring what she promises. It's not her fault. I know she tries her very best to make every wish come true, but sometimes there are wishes that just aren't meant to come true."

Lucy's eyes grew damp with tears. "Mine *will* come true," she said fiercely. "I know it will. Daddy told me that if I was good, and if I wished hard enough for something, and really, truly believed I would get it, then I would.''

All very well for Daddy to say, Sherrie thought bitterly. "And I'm sure you will get your wish one day, sweetheart," she replied, trying desperately to think of the right thing to say. "But it might not come true by this Christmas."

"Why not?" A tear welled up and spilled from the corner of Lucy's eye. "I waited such a long time. I don't want to wait anymore."

Hating herself for raising such a false hope in the little girl's heart, Sherrie felt her own heart breaking. She wouldn't be able to sleep if she left the child upset like this. "Well," she said, sending up a silent prayer of her own, "perhaps Mrs. Claus can make a miracle happen after all. We'll just have to wait and see."

"I know she will." Lucy sniffed, only partly comforted.

Sherrie reached for a tissue from the bedside table and dabbed at the little girl's nose. Then she folded her arms around her and gave her a warm hug. "Don't worry, sweetheart. Miracles can happen at Christmastime. You'll see. Now Daddy is going to come up and read you a story. Which one would you like?"

She found the book that Lucy asked for and laid it on the table. Then she gave the child a swift kiss on the forehead and hurried from the room. She'd had all she could take for the moment.

She was only making things worse by raising Lucy's hopes like that. The sad thing was, both Matt and his daughter needed a woman in their lives. Matt was obviously lonely. That was the reason he'd acted so impulsively earlier. Christmas was the very worst time to be lonely. Elaine had been right about that.

To make matters worse, Sherrie told herself gloomily as she went back into the kitchen to clean up, she was beginning to seriously wish she could fill the role as Lucy's mother. Which was impossible, of course. Matt and Lucy needed someone far more capable than she would ever be. She couldn't be more wrong for him if she tried, and he knew it.

So now she was faced once more with the impossible task of finding a woman who was right for him. The fact that she was just beginning to realize how much he and Lucy meant to her would make the task that much more difficult.

Sherrie rinsed out dishes and stacked them into the dishwasher, trying to resolve the furious argument going on inside her head. On the one hand, she would rather die than introduce a prospective wife to Matthew Blanchard. On the other hand, she would die inside if she didn't at least make every effort to grant Lucy her wish.

Oh, she could think of a dozen reasons why Maria Benitto wasn't the right one for Matt, and every one of them selfish. She would invite Maria over for dinner, she decided. Maybe even talk her into making scampi for Matt. He would love that. After that, it would be up to the two of them to take it from there. At least she would be satisfied she had done her very best.

The next day, instead of searching for a new apartment, Sherrie gave Maria a call. When she learned that Sherrie would be in the neighborhood, her ex-neighbor immediately invited her over for dinner. It didn't take long for Sherrie to convince Maria to come over to Matt's house on Sunday night.

"Scampi is his very favorite dinner," she told Maria as they sat enjoying a rich-flavored coffee after dinner. "I know the last thing you want to do is cook for someone else on your night off, but I'll be happy to pay you, of course. I think it would be a wonderful surprise for Matt. Sort of an early Christmas present."

Maria raised her eyebrows and gave her a long look.

"And Lucy, too, of course," Sherrie added hurriedly.

"I can give you the recipe," Maria said, brushing a crumb from her ample bosom. "It really isn't that difficult."

"I'm not that good at following recipes," Sherrie admitted with a sigh.

"Most recipes are easy enough to follow. All you have to do is concentrate, read the directions and take it a step at a time."

"You don't know what a klutz I am," Sherrie said darkly. "I could ruin a ham sandwich." She recounted the incident with the champagne cork, making Maria laugh so hard she gasped for breath.

"Well, I'll be happy to come over and show you how to cook scampi," she said when she could talk again. "That way, you'll be able to do it yourself the next time."

Sherrie didn't know whether to feel pleased or miserable about the success of her new plan. Driving back to the house later that night, she told herself she was doing the right thing for Lucy's sake.

After all, there were no guarantees that Matt and Maria would fall for each other. In fact, the more she thought about it, the more she doubted that the two of them had much in common, except an appreciation for good food. She was, however, committed now, and she would just have to leave the outcome up to the Fates.

She arrived at the Blanchards' house just as Matt was opening the front door. He and Lucy waited in the doorway for her while she parked the car and ran up the driveway. Although the rain had stopped, the east wind sang in the branches of the firs, bringing a promise of early snow.

It would be nice to have a white Christmas, she thought as she greeted Lucy with a warm smile. "Hi, sweetheart. How was the show?"

Lucy was eager to tell her all about it, and dragged her into the house talking nonstop. Sherrie barely had time to exchange a glance with Matt, and she couldn't judge his mood from his expression.

He seemed relieved when Sherrie offered to bathe Lucy and put her to bed. Thinking he must be tired, she didn't expect to see him when she went downstairs again, but he called out to her as she passed the living-room door.

He was sitting in his favorite armchair, with the newspaper spread out on his knees, when she went into the room. "Did Lucy settle down all right?" he asked as she sank onto a chair by the fireplace.

"She was asleep before I finished tucking her in," Sherrie said, smiling at the memory.

"Then I guess I won't disturb her with a story tonight." He cleared his throat and shook the pages of the newspaper before carefully folding it.

"I don't think she'll hear it if you do," Sherrie murmured, wondering why he appeared to be so nervous.

"Well, it's just as well. I wanted to talk to you about something."

So that was why he was so uncomfortable, Sherrie thought. He was going to set her straight about last night. Although she'd been expecting it, she could feel her stomach knotting up as she waited for him to get it off his chest.

"It's...er...about last night," Matt said, looking everywhere but at her.

Sherrie did her best to look surprised. "Last night?"

"Yes, I shouldn't have...that is...I should have..."

"If you're talking about that little kiss you gave me," Sherrie said, airily waving her hand in dismissal, "I'd forgotten all about it. After all, it was just a friendly gesture in the spirit of the holiday season, right?"

He looked taken aback. "Right," he echoed uncertainly.

"Well, then, there's nothing to worry about, is there?"

This time he firmly met her gaze. "I guess not."

His voice, dropping to that husky murmur, almost destroyed her composure. She was about to get up and make her escape when he added, "Tomorrow is Saturday."

"Yes," she said warily. "I know."

"We'll be pretty busy at the store over the weekend, and Lucy won't be in kindergarten."

"I've been wondering about that." She hesitated, not sure how he'd take her idea.

He gave her a questioning look. "If you have any suggestions," he said quietly, "I'm anxious to hear them."

"I was wondering how you'd feel about making Lucy my assistant for the day. We could dress her as an elf and she could hand out the candy canes. I think she'd enjoy that."

Matt turned his gaze toward the fire, and appeared to be giving the idea some intense thought. "You'd have to keep an eye on her as well as deal with the other kids," he said at last. "Are you sure you want the added responsibility?"

"I'd love it," Sherrie assured him. "It will be fun for both of us."

Matt sat back in his chair and looked at her for a long moment, until she could feel every inch of her skin tingling. Then he said softly, "Thank you, Sherrie. I really don't know what I would have done without you."

She held her gaze, although it was difficult to do with her entire body aching to throw herself into his arms and beg him to make wild, passionate love to her. "I should be thanking you," she said unsteadily. "The holidays would have been very lonely and depressing for me all by myself in Tom's apartment. You've given me a home for the holidays, and I'm grateful."

His mouth curved in a wry smile. "It's not much of a vacation for you, is it?"

She shrugged. "I don't mind. It keeps my mind off my own problems."

"Your ex-fiancé was a fool. Perhaps he'll come to his senses and realize that."

Taken aback, she dropped her gaze. "I hope not," she said, her voice low. "I realize now what a big mistake marrying Jason would have been. I just wish I'd seen it earlier. I could have saved us both a great deal of heartache and embarrassment."

"The important thing is to learn from mistakes. Not to make the same one twice."

So there it was, she thought, keeping her gaze determinedly on the fire. A clear and precise warning. Well, he didn't have to tell her twice. Summoning a fake yawn, she got to her feet. "I guess it's time I went to bed." She escaped through the door before he'd finished answering her.

# Chapter Eight

It wasn't until she was lying in bed that she remembered she hadn't mentioned inviting Maria over. Maybe it was better that way, she thought as she turned on her side for the umpteenth time. Although Matt had told her she could invite whomever she wanted, she didn't want to give him the chance to find an excuse why she couldn't have Maria over.

It would be better to surprise him, she decided. He could hardly object when Maria presented him with his favorite meal, served by a professional cook, just the way he liked it. That would certainly gain her points right from the start.

Although the prospect of Matt getting together with Maria depressed her, she was determined to go through with it. She owed it to Lucy, she reminded herself. Even so, it took her a long time to fall asleep.

She awoke the next morning without her usual bounce and vigor. Matt had already left for the store when she went downstairs with Lucy. He'd left almost an hour earlier than usual, and Sherrie couldn't help wondering if he was making a point of avoiding her.

As always, however, visiting with all the children soon put things back into perspective again. Lucy seemed to enjoy her task of handing out the candy canes, and told everyone that Mrs. Claus was her very best friend.

By the end of the afternoon shift, Sherrie had convinced herself that she was doing what was best for everyone. So what if she couldn't have Matt Blanchard. She didn't need a man in her life to be happy. She was used to living alone, and preferred it that way.

When she lived on her own she didn't have the constant worry about cooking the right meals, running the right errands or making the right decisions. All she had to do was please herself. It was a much more relaxing way to live. She ignored the part of her mind that kept insisting it was also a lonely way to live.

Lucy seemed quite disappointed when Sherrie told her it was time to go find her daddy. "Have you found my mommy yet?" she asked, destroying Sherrie's hopes that she wasn't going to mention it.

"Not yet, sweetheart, but I'm still working on it. We still have a lot of days before Christmas."

Lucy nodded. "I don't really need a mommy until Christmas, 'cause Sherrie is staying with us." Her smile faded, and her shoulders slumped. "I wanted Sherrie to be my mommy," she said quietly, "but she has to go away after Christmas."

Sherrie's throat tightened. "I'm sure she'll be sad about that. I know I would be."

"I'll be sad, too." For a moment Lucy looked about ready to burst into tears. Then she looked up, her face full of hope. "But it will be fun having a new mommy to play with."

"You bet it will." Sherrie gave the little girl a hug. "Now you'd better go to your daddy. He's waiting over in the toy department."

Lucy obediently slipped from her lap. "I do wish you could be my mommy," she said wistfully.

"So do I." Sherrie cleared her throat. "But you wouldn't like it at the North Pole. It's very cold and lonely there."

"It's lonely here, too," Lucy said, sounding much older than her years.

"I know, sweetheart." Sherrie blinked hard as she watched the child run down to the toy department and grasp her father by the hand.

Lucy talked earnestly to him as they made their way to the elevators, and neither one of them spared a glance for Mrs. Claus, who sat in her red velvet chair, doing her best not to smudge her mascara.

Saturday seemed to drag by for Sherrie, though Lucy appeared to enjoy every single moment of her job as Mrs. Claus's elf. She stood close to Sherrie's side, listening to all the children while they talked to Mrs. Claus, an expression of rapt attention on her face.

Later, however, she seemed unusually quiet on the way back to the house. Sherrie wondered anxiously if the child was coming down with a cold. She seemed to brighten, however, when Sherrie told her they were expecting a visitor for dinner the next day.

That evening Matt announced he was going to his health club, and would grab something to eat while he was out. Sherrie cooked hamburgers for herself and Lucy, and although she chatted with the child, her heart wasn't in it. Her mind kept wandering back to Matt, wondering what he was doing.

Sunday was a busy day at the store, and once more Lucy was on hand to help Mrs. Claus greet the children. Sherrie was anxious for the day to be over, so she could put her plan into action.

Maria arrived promptly that evening, bringing with her the ingredients for the meal. Sherrie greeted her with her usual enthusiasm, though she was beginning to feel nervous about Matt's reaction to his unexpected guest.

Maria soon put Sherrie to work preparing the ingredients for the scampi. Lucy, apparently fascinated by this plump, lively woman with the hearty laugh, insisted on helping, too.

Maria gave the little girl a bowl and showed her how to beat the egg yolks, salt and sugar for the dessert.

Following her friend's instructions, Sherrie peeled shrimp, crushed garlic, grated lemons and chopped parsley.

"We'll serve it over rice," Maria said, opening a package.

Sherrie looked at her in alarm. "I can't cook rice. It always comes out lumpy and sticky."

"That's because you let the water go off the boil."

"Here's Daddy!" Lucy called out, abandoning her beating to rush out of the kitchen.

Sherrie's stomach took a nosedive. It was now or never. "I'll be back in a minute," she said, "and I'll introduce you to Matt. I think you'll like him."

Maria nodded cheerfully, and took over Lucy's job of beating the eggs.

Matt stood in the hall, listening to Lucy's excited chatter when Sherrie went to meet him. He looked up as she approached, eyeing her warily. "Lucy tells me we have a guest for dinner."

"I was going to ask you if it was okay, but you weren't in the office when I got there," Sherrie said, doing her best to look innocent.

Matt took off his raincoat and hung it in the closet. Somehow the hallway always seemed smaller when he was standing there with her, Sherrie thought as she waited for his reaction.

He closed the closet, then looked down at her with a dubious expression on his face. "Another friend of yours, I take it."

"Her name is Maria, and she's helping me cook your favorite dinner," Sherrie said defensively.

"I see," Matt said.

Sherrie had the uncomfortable feeling that he meant it literally. "I'd like you to meet her." She turned toward the kitchen, then looked back over her shoulder at him. "I hope you don't mind. You did say—"

"I don't mind," Matt said quietly.

Unconvinced by his tone, Sherrie led him back to the kitchen. When she opened the door, the wonderful aroma of fresh lemons and garlic greeted her. She hoped Matt would be suitably impressed.

Maria looked up, the bowl held firmly in her arm as she expertly whisked the eggs. At the sight of Matt her chubby face broke into a wide smile. Her dark eyes flicked over his lean figure, obviously enjoying what they saw. "This must be Matt," she said, wiping her hands on her apron.

Sherrie quickly introduced them. "Maria is a sous-chef at a very good Italian restaurant," she said after Matt had shaken Maria's plump hand. "I thought it would be a treat to have her help me cook scampi for you."

Matt's cool blue gaze settled on her face. "That was very thoughtful of you, Sherrie."

He seemed annoyed with her, Sherrie thought uneasily. Maybe this wasn't such a hot idea, after all. "Well," she said awkwardly, "why don't you go watch television with Lucy, and I'll give you a call when dinner is ready."

"I'll do that." Matt bestowed one of his smiles on Maria, then led Lucy from the kitchen.

"Mmm, quite a dish," Maria said with a chuckle, after the door had closed behind them. "I can see why you want to impress him."

Sherrie flushed. "I just wanted to make up for the last two dinners I cooked."

"Sure you did, honey," Maria said, patting her arm. "Don't worry, I won't tell him how you feel. Though I tell you, if you don't let him know soon, you could lose him. A man like that doesn't stay lonely for long."

Sherrie took a deep breath. "Maria, you've got it all wrong. I'm not in the least bit interested in Matt. After what happened to me I couldn't care less about men. I just wanted to do something nice for him and Lucy, that's all."

Maria shrugged. "Okay, whatever you say. Now we'd better get this custard cooked so we can chill it before we eat it."

Trying to rid herself of the uneasy squirming in her stomach, Sherrie concentrated on the task. The meal was surprisingly simple under Maria's detailed direction. Within half an hour the custard was chilling in the fridge, and Sherrie had the beautifully cooked shrimp laid out enticingly on its bed of rice.

"You see?" Maria said, as she surveyed the results of Sherrie's efforts. "All you needed was a little confidence in yourself. It's amazing what you can achieve when you really try."

Sherrie had to agree. "I've surprised myself," she said, feeling a little burst of pleasure. "I don't usually go by recipes because they always look so complicated. It's easier to use mixes and frozen dinners."

"Ugh!" Maria shuddered. "Come on, let's get this on the table before it gets cold."

Matt and Lucy had already devoured the minestrone soup that Maria had brought along with her, left over from the previous night's menu at the restaurant.

Sherrie could hardly wait to lay the shrimp platter on the table. Matt's exclamation of pleasure was worth every second she'd spent hovering anxiously over the stove.

As she watched him sample the first mouthful of scampi, she thought she could hardly stand the suspense. Then she let out her breath in relief when she saw the look of delight on his face.

"The best scampi I've ever tasted," he said, giving her a warm smile.

It took a second or two for her to remember why she'd arranged this dinner. Her pleasure evaporated like a deflating balloon. "It's Maria's recipe," she said, trying to sound enthusiastic. "She showed me how to do it. She really is a wonderful cook."

"Ah, but you did all the work," Maria said pointedly. "I couldn't have done better myself." She looked across the table at Matt. "Wait until you taste the zabaglione."

"What's zabalony?" Lucy asked.

"It's a custard," Sherrie explained. "And that's Maria's recipe, too." She glanced at Matt, but he seemed preoccupied with his dinner. In fact, he hardly uttered a word throughout the rest of the meal. By the time Sherrie served the custard, she was so apprehensive she almost tipped his glass over as she set it in front of him.

Lucy loved the dessert. Luckily she kept asking Maria questions, keeping the woman's attention off the silent man at the head of the table.

Another miserable failure, Sherrie thought as she helped Maria clear away the dishes after the meal. No woman would be interested in a man who totally ignored her for the entire evening.

At least Matt had the grace to thank Maria for her part in cooking the wonderful meal, and even offered to bathe Lucy and put her to bed so that Sherrie could spend a little more time with her friend.

Even so, Sherrie felt so bad about Matt's indifference, she felt compelled to apologize to Maria.

"Don't worry about it," Maria said, giving Sherrie a hug. "He was just tired, that's all. I can tell you one thing, though, he enjoyed his meal. There's a man who loves his food, all right."

"Thanks to you." Sherrie held out an envelope to her. "I couldn't have done it without you."

Maria shook her head. "Put your money away, honey. I enjoyed it. It was a treat to eat with a family again. Besides, you did all the work. Now I have to get home. I have a busy day tomorrow."

Sherrie followed her into the hallway, struggling with her mixed feelings. Maria would have been a wonderful mother to Lucy. It was obvious she adored children, and Lucy had clung to her before being whisked off to bed.

And if Matt hadn't been so unsociable, she thought fiercely, he would have realized what an attractive, warmhearted, spirited woman Maria was. She would have been a fabulous companion for him.

Matt was making her mission incredibly difficult. Yet a part of her couldn't help rejoicing in the fact that no matter how suitable Maria might seem, Matt just wasn't interested. In fact, she was beginning to seriously doubt if Matthew Blanchard would ever be interested in any woman.

The night air chilled her to the bone as she stood outside with Maria. It was a clear night, with a bright, white moon on the wane overhead. The air smelled frosty, and the wind rattled the branches of the tall firs.

"Wouldn't be surprised if we get some snow," Maria remarked as she tucked her hands into warm gloves. She climbed into her car and rolled down the window. Looking up at Sherrie, she smiled. "I left the recipes on the counter. Now you can cook your man scampi anytime he wants it."

"I told you, he's not my man," Sherrie said hotly.

Maria shook her head. "You know, Sherrie, if you say it often enough, you'll get to believe it. And what a waste that would be." She rolled up the window before Sherrie could ask her what she meant by that cryptic remark.

Going back into the welcome warmth of the house, Sherrie shivered as she closed the door. At least the night hadn't been a total disaster, she thought as she hurried back to the kitchen. The dinner had been the best meal she'd ever cooked. Maybe she wasn't such a klutz after all.

Browsing through the cookbooks on the shelf, she found one on Italian cooking. All she had to do, she told herself, was to concentrate the way she had tonight. Excitement stirred as she read through the recipes. Some of the meals looked simple enough. They would be fun to try.

She gave a guilty start as the kitchen door suddenly opened. Matt stood in the doorway, and his expression threw a dark blanket over her enthusiasm.

"I want to talk to you," he said in a voice that warned her not to argue.

She lifted her chin. "What about?"

"About your friend, Maria. And Elaine. I get the distinct feeling that you are trying to play matchmaker."

Sherrie's heart thumped. "I don't know what you mean."

Matt stepped into the kitchen and closed the door behind him. "Oh, yes, you do. You have been in my house for only five days, and in that short time you've managed to introduce me to two of your friends. How many more do you have lined up in the wings?"

"No one." She met his gaze squarely. "No one you'd be interested in, anyway."

Matt lifted his face to the ceiling and swore. "Dammit, Sherrie, I have enough problems as it is with women. As far as I'm concerned, most of them are far more interested in my money than they are in me, and I really don't appreciate coming home at the end of a hard day to find some strange woman sizing me up as a possible meal ticket. So just do me a favor and let your friends find their own damn men."

"I wasn't doing it for them," Sherrie burst out. "I was doing it for Lucy."

Matt stared at her, while the seconds ticked by in ominous silence. "Lucy?" he repeated finally, sounding as if he'd never heard the name before.

"Yes, Lucy." Sherrie turned away from him and began stacking dishes noisily into the dishwasher. "When I was talking to her as Mrs. Claus, she told me that she had only one wish. She wanted a mommy for Christmas. I told her I'd do what I could to find her one.''

"Oh, good Lord."

Sherrie picked up a pan and began to scrub, willing herself not to give in to tears.

After another long pause, Matt said quietly, "I know how fond you are of my daughter, but I'm afraid she is going to be bitterly disappointed. If and when I should start looking for a wife, and I have no intention of doing so in the foreseeable future, I'll be the one to decide who qualifies for that role. So from now on, I'd appreciate it if you would mind your own business and let me get on with mine.''

Sherrie winced as she heard the door shut a little too hard. Carefully she placed the pan in the dishwasher. She'd really made a mess of things this time, she thought gloomily. Tom was right. She was too irresponsible for her own good.

She should never have made such a rash promise to Lucy. She certainly shouldn't have told Matt about it. Now he was really mad at her, and she was going to break Lucy's heart.

She lifted her face and closed her eyes as a tear drifted down her cheek. Softly she whispered, "Merry Christmas, klutz."

Matt sat in the living room, staring into the flickering flames of the gas fire. He hadn't moved in the past hour, and still he couldn't seem to calm his chaotic thoughts.

He wanted to take Sherrie Latimer by the shoulders and shake her until her teeth rattled. She was an interfering little busybody with snowballs for brains. How she had the nerve to tell his daughter she'd find her a mother he couldn't imagine. It didn't occur to her that he might not want a wife. Even if he did, what gave Miss Fairy Godmother the idea she could pick one out for him?

Matt threw his newspaper down on the floor in disgust. He should have known she'd be trouble the minute he saw her sitting on the chair swinging those ridiculous high-heeled shoes. He'd brought all this on himself, by not listening to his better judgment.

Surging to his feet, Matt glanced at the clock. He had to get to bed or he'd have a head full of cotton in the morning. Though he seriously doubted he would get any sleep.

He trod quietly up the stairs, aware of every creak. What irritated him most of all was the knowledge that part of his anger stemmed from his guilt. He didn't like Sherrie Latimer reminding him that he was depriving Lucy of the one thing in the world she wanted the most.

He'd managed to convince himself that it was better for his daughter not to risk the heartbreak of losing another mother. Yet deep down he knew it was his own fear of heartbreak that had kept him from taking another chance on love.

Thanks to Miss Latimer, he'd been forced to face that fact tonight, and it wasn't easy to swallow. To make matters worse, he was uncomfortably aware that his anger toward Sherrie wasn't due to her interference as much as it was due to her casual indifference to his feelings.

Vigorously brushing his teeth in the bathroom, Matt tried to avoid the disturbing facts. Sherrie Latimer was beginning to get under his skin. So much so that all he could think about lately was how much he wanted to kiss her again. Not only kiss her, but take her into his bed and make love to her all night, until his strength gave out.

Much as he hated to acknowledge the fact, he'd been hurt when she'd acted so nonchalant about the kiss he'd given her. True, it had been a stupid impulse, and he should have known better than to give in to it. But if he was honest with himself, he'd be forced to admit he'd enjoyed it immensely. More than he should have, actually. He'd rather hoped that Sherrie had enjoyed it, too.

Instead she'd tossed the whole thing off as meaningless, making him feel like the office jerk going around stealing kisses under the mistletoe. God knows what she'd do if she knew the kind of thoughts that went through his head every time he laid eyes on her.

Impatiently he threw down the toothbrush and left the bathroom. He was a grown man, supposedly well able to handle rejection. It was simply his pride taking a beating, he told himself as he climbed into bed.

Even so, he couldn't quite rid himself of the depression he felt at the thought of Sherrie calmly and dispassionately picking out another woman to be his wife. Or the loneliness he felt lying in that empty bed, his body aching for the warm touch of a woman who just happened to look like Sherrie Latimer. And that was what worried him most of all.

Sherrie slept badly that night, and woke up the next morning with a headache. At first she couldn't remember why she felt so down, then it all came back to her. Somehow she would have to tell Lucy not to expect a new mom for Christmas.

She would have to pick the right time, she decided, and first thing in the morning was definitely not it. Once again Matt had left early, and Lucy, for some reason, seemed determined to dawdle over everything. She barely made it to the kindergarten in time for the bell.

Sherrie had planned on doing some Christmas shopping before changing into her Mrs. Claus costume, but somehow this morning she couldn't seem to concentrate on anything.

Lucy's gift would be easy to pick out since she already had several ideas in mind. It was Matt's gift that was giving her problems. She wanted something special, something unusual. Wandering through a men's clothing store in the mall, she glanced at the tables loaded with socks and ties, and a host of various little gadgets done up in Christmas packaging. Nothing seemed right.

Her visit to the sporting goods store proved no more successful. Staring at rows of golf balls stacked neatly on the shelf, Sherrie realized she didn't even know if Matt played golf. It would be too obvious to ask him now.

A quick glance at her watch told her she had only a few minutes to get back to Blanchard's and change. A crowd of shoppers stood in front of the elevators, and she decided not to wait around for one. It would be quicker to take the escalator up the three floors to the sixth.

As she stepped off on the fourth floor, a young woman handed her a folder. Sherrie took it, barely glancing at it before slipping it into her purse. She made a mental note to look at it later, then promptly forgot about it in her rush to get changed into her Mrs. Claus clothes.

Later that morning, as she sat sipping a cup of coffee with Beryl in the cafeteria, she was hunting through her purse for a tissue when she saw the folder again.

She took it out and opened it up. It was an advertisement for a special on painted portraits. She was about to crumple it up when Beryl leaned forward to take a look at it.

"That's Angela Danvers," she said, pointing to the picture on the front of the folder. "She's the artist who paints the portraits. She's very good at it, too."

Sherrie studied the picture. The artist was a slim, elegant woman with sleek blond hair pulled back in a bright red ribbon. Her delicate features were carefully made up, and she wore a striking blue-and-silver sweater over a long, black skirt.

"She owns the art gallery on Sadler Street," Beryl said, picking up her coffee cup. "Her husband died about three years ago, and left her to run it. She paints portraits as a sideline. I guess business isn't that great at the gallery."

Sherrie stared at the folder as the glimmer of an idea took shape. "How long does it take her to paint a portrait?" she asked casually.

"I don't know. A few hours, I guess." Beryl looked at her curiously. "Are you thinking of getting one done?"

"I just might." Sherrie stuffed the folder back into her purse. "I have a phone call to make, so I'd better run. I'll see you later." She left before Beryl could ask any more questions, and headed back to the lounge to use the phone. Angela Danvers herself answered the call. "It will take about two weeks to paint the portrait," she told Sherrie. "I'll need about ten hours of sitting time with the subject."

Sherrie did some quick calculations. "Can you do one for me in time for Christmas?" she asked hopefully.

She held her breath through the short pause that followed. "Actually," Angela Danvers said, "I'm booking sittings for next year. I don't usually work this close to Christmas. My gallery keeps me fairly busy this time of year."

"I see," Sherrie said, making no effort to hide her disappointment. "Well, thank you for your time."

She was about to hang up when the artist asked carefully, "Was it going to be a Christmas gift?"

"Yes," Sherrie said with a heavy sigh. "A very special gift for a very special person."

"Well, why don't you give the recipient a Christmas card telling him what you plan to do, then you can arrange a sitting later on? I'm sure he'll be happy to wait for a portrait of you."

"Oh, it's not my portrait I want," Sherrie said. "It's a portrait of his daughter. I wanted it to be a surprise at Christmas." Before she knew it she was telling the kind, understanding voice on the phone the whole story of how she'd messed things up for Matt and Lucy, and how she wanted to do something special to make up for it.

"Well, maybe I can squeeze it in," Angela Danvers said, when she was finished. "If you can arrange to have the little girl here at my house for an hour or so in the evening for the next two weeks, I should be able to get it done in time for Christmas."

Sherrie's spirits dropped again. "I don't think her father will let me take her out every evening. Could we make it in the afternoons?"

"I'm sorry, Sherrie, but I have to take care of the gallery during the day. If you want the portrait before Christmas, it will have to be evenings."

Sherrie sighed again. It looked as if her marvelous idea was doomed, after all. By the time she cooked dinner, it would be too late to take Lucy across town for an hour or more, even if Matt would agree.

An idea occurred to her just then, a daring idea that might well backfire if Matt got wind of it. Sherrie hesitated then, as usual, threw caution to the wind. She had little left to lose now, anyway. She might as well go for broke.

# *Chapter Nine*

"I don't suppose you'd consider coming to the house for the sittings?" Sherrie asked tentatively. Matt would probably kill her for arranging it, she thought with a pang of apprehension, but once it was set up he wouldn't have a lot of choice in the matter.

"I could do that, I suppose," Angela said doubtfully. "But then it wouldn't be much of a surprise for Lucy's father."

Her spirits rising, Sherrie thought furiously. "Well, I don't have to tell him the portrait is for him. I could say I won the portrait in a draw, and that I wanted a portrait of Lucy for myself. Then I'll just wrap it and put it under the tree for him."

"That might work." Angela uttered a low, musical laugh. "You must think a lot of this man to go to all this trouble."

"He's been very kind to me," Sherrie said quickly. "When can we expect you for the first sitting, then?"

After finalizing the arrangements, she hung up, her excitement growing. This would be the perfect gift for Matt. Something really special. Something no one else would give him.

Feeling immensely pleased with herself, she went back down to the fifth floor and settled herself in Mrs. Claus's red chair.

Lucy arrived a little later than normal that afternoon. Her usual smile was missing, and she looked as if she had something serious on her mind as she climbed onto Mrs. Claus's lap.

Sherrie watched the little girl as she sat plucking at the pleats in her red tartan skirt. "What's the matter, sweetheart?" she asked, when Lucy showed no sign of talking. "Aren't you feeling well?"

Lucy looked up, and her face was full of accusation. "Bonnie says that you're not really Mrs. Claus."

Sherrie looked at her in dismay. That was all she needed. If Lucy lost her belief in Santa, Matt was likely to blame his substitute.

She looked down at Lucy's dejected face and did her best to smile. "Well, I guess Bonnie doesn't know everything. Of course I'm Mrs. Claus. Just ask all those little kids out there." She nodded at the straggly line of children waiting to talk to her. "They'll tell you who I am."

"You haven't found me a mommy yet," Lucy said, fixing wide blue eyes on her face. "If you were Mrs. Claus, you could find me a mommy."

Sherrie swallowed. Now was definitely not the time to tell the little girl the truth. "It's not Christmas yet," she said, feeling more than a little desperate. "Anyway, I have a surprise for you."

Lucy still looked sulky. "What kind of surprise?"

"A special surprise. A really nice lady is going to come to the house tonight. She's going to paint your picture."

Lucy's eyes widened. "Really? Is she going to stay with us?"

"Well, just for the evening."

Lucy's face dropped, and Sherrie added hurriedly, "But she's going to be there every evening for a week or two, so you'll have lots of time to spend with her. She's a really nice lady."

To her relief, Lucy's face brightened considerably. "Is she a special lady?"

Sherrie thought about how Angela had put herself out to do this for her. "A very special lady," she said solemnly.

"Does Daddy know about the lady?"

Sherrie's heart skipped nervously. "Er...no, sweetheart, not yet. Perhaps you'd better let me explain about that, okay?"

Lucy nodded cheerfully. "Okay. It will be a big surprise."

A very big surprise, Sherrie thought anxiously. Maybe this time she'd better warn him in advance that she was expecting company, instead of springing it on him.

She had no chance to talk to him until she went to pick up Lucy from his office later. Matt looked up as she walked in, and to her relief he seemed to have forgotten his anger of the night before.

"Lucy is downstairs with Beryl," he said as she glanced around the empty room. "She wanted to do some Christmas shopping, so I asked Beryl to take her."

Sherrie looked at him in dismay. "I could have taken her if she'd asked me."

"She wants to pick out something for you," Matt said gently.

Her disappointment melted in a rush of warmth. "Really? That's so sweet."

"Don't get too excited." Matt put down his pen and leaned back in his chair. "Lucy has some weird and wonderful tastes. Last year she bought me a green fur hat with a bright red feather stuck in the hatband. I felt like Robin Hood."

Sherrie grinned, trying to picture the suave and sophisticated Matthew Blanchard in a green fur hat. "Thanks for the warning."

He didn't return the grin. In fact, he seemed to be on edge. He dropped his gaze and picked up the pen, flipping it back and forth through his fingers. "I had a phone call from Mrs. Halloway this morning," he said finally.

Her stomach felt hollow as she watched him. "How is her mother?"

"She's improving. Mrs. Halloway doesn't want to leave her until after Christmas, though."

Relief made her want to cheer out loud. "Well, I can understand that."

"The store will be closed early Christmas Eve, and Christmas Day, of course," Matt said, still not looking at her.

"Yes, of course." She frowned, wondering what he was trying to tell her.

He glanced up at her, then shifted his gaze back to the pen again. "I just wondered, I mean—" He broke off, muttering a soft curse under his breath.

Now she was really getting concerned. She moved closer to the desk. "Is something wrong?"

"No." He seemed to make up his mind about something. "Look, I don't know what plans you had for Christmas Day. Mrs. Halloway always spent Christmas with her mother, since I stay home to take care of Lucy between Christmas and New Year's. I just wanted to let you know that your obligation ends on Christmas Eve."

"I see." She could hardly speak past the hard lump in her throat. "I'll bring my things to the store that day, then. I can go home from there." Home where? she wondered. To Tom's empty apartment? The thought was like a cold, damp hand squeezing her heart.

"Well, as a matter of fact—" Matt broke off as the door opened and Lucy burst in.

"Hi, Daddy," she yelled, "you'll never guess what I got for—" She saw Sherrie and shut off her words with her hand over her mouth.

Beryl appeared in the doorway behind her. "We had to wait to get them wrapped," she said, her arms full of packages. "Where do you want me to put them?"

"You can give them to Sherrie," Matt said, "she can take them home and put them under the tree."

Sherrie took the packages from Beryl and thanked her.

"My pleasure," Beryl said, grinning. "Merry Christmas." She went off, leaving Sherrie wondering what Lucy had bought that was so amusing.

"We don't have a tree," Lucy said pointedly.

"We will have one by tonight." Matt smiled at his daughter. "I'm stopping off to get one on the way home." He glanced over at Sherrie, the smile still on his face. "I thought we could all decorate the tree tonight."

"Yay!" Lucy shouted, jumping up and down in excitement.

Sherrie almost groaned aloud. She still hadn't told Matt about Angela Danvers. "I'm afraid Lucy and I are going to be a little busy tonight," she said.

Lucy stopped dancing around, while Matt gave her a suspicious look. "Busy?"

"Yes." With her fingers crossed behind her, she launched into her story of winning the portrait in a draw. "I was going to turn it down," she said, her voice getting more and more uncertain as she watched Matt's face darken. "I didn't want a portrait of myself—that's so pretentious—and I don't have anyone to give it to, except Tom, and he'd laugh his head off at the thought of hanging a picture of me on the wall—"

"Get to the point," Matt said grimly when she paused for breath.

"Well, I thought it would be nice to have a portrait of Lucy to keep," Sherrie finished lamely. "It would be a reminder of one of the nicest Christmas holidays I've ever spent."

His face softened a fraction at that. "All right. How long will it take to paint the portrait? Where does Lucy have to go for the sittings?"

Sherrie hesitated. While she was still working out how to answer him, Lucy said impatiently, "The lady's coming to our house to paint it. Mrs. Claus says she's a very special lady."

"Aha!" Matt said, a dangerous gleam appearing in his eye. "I guessed as much."

Sherrie's heart sank all the way to her high-heeled shoes. He thought she was matchmaking again. She should have anticipated that. "It's not what you think," she said, lifting her chin. "I really do want a portrait of Lucy to keep."

Matt nodded. "Uh-huh. And the artist is a very special lady who will be spending several hours in my home."

"An hour or so in the evenings," Sherrie protested. "I can assure you, she will be busy painting Lucy's portrait."

"You bet she will." Matt leaned his elbows on the desk and fixed his intent blue gaze on her face. "I'll make sure of that."

"Can she help us put the stuff on the tree?" Lucy asked eagerly.

"I don't think so," Sherrie said quickly. "I think we'd better go now, and leave your dad to get on with his work."

She left the office with a strong feeling that she hadn't heard the last of Matt's suspicions. At least this time she was completely innocent. Somehow she'd have to convince him of that, she thought as she drove Lucy back to the house. Something told her it wasn't going to be easy.

She'd planned a simple casserole that evening, which was just as well, since Matt arrived home later than usual. Lucy was bubbling with excitement throughout the meal, chattering almost nonstop, making normal conversation difficult. Sherrie still hadn't had a chance to talk to Matt when the doorbell announced the arrival of Angela Danvers.

The artist was even more impressive than her picture. She wore a small rhinestone clasp in her sleek blond hair instead of the ribbon, and a simple black sweater over clinging black pants.

Angela Danvers had the kind of lithe figure she would kill for, Sherrie thought as she took the elegant woman's coat. The echo of an expensive and exotic perfume drifted behind the slender body as Angela followed an eager Lucy to the living room.

Bringing up the rear, Sherrie felt herself growing tense as she wondered how Matt would react to this glamorous creature. She just hoped he wouldn't be rude.

"This is Angela Danvers," she said belatedly as Matt rose from his chair by the fire.

"Charmed, I'm sure," Angela murmured, extending her long, delicate fingers in Matt's direction.

Her greeting was so classic Continental Sherrie half expected Matt to bow low over the woman's hand and kiss the back of it. Instead he gave the hand a casual shake and let it go.

"This is a wonderful room," Angela said, looking around her with an air of appreciation. "That paneling would make the perfect backdrop for the portrait."

"Actually," Matt said, giving the artist one of his devastating smiles, "I think perhaps the dining room might be better. I'm going to be setting up the tree in here, and I don't want to distract you."

"Oh, you won't distract me," Angela said with a lilting laugh. "I'm used to people wandering around while I paint."

"I would prefer you use the dining room," Matt said pleasantly.

Sherrie cringed, but Angela appeared unruffled by his insistence. "Well, of course, if that's what you wish." She looked down at Lucy and gave her a brilliant smile. "All right, honey, why don't you show me where the dining room is?"

"I'll show you," Sherrie said, giving Matt a reproachful look. Angela Danvers was being utterly charming, and he, as usual, was being awkward.

She left the room with the artist and Lucy, who seemed a little in awe of this new acquaintance. Angela surveyed the dining room with a critical eye, then announced that it would do just fine.

Sherrie helped her carry in her equipment, then while the artist was setting up, she took Lucy upstairs to put on a dress that she'd bought her especially for the portrait.

She had to admit, when she saw Lucy wearing it, that her choice couldn't have been better. Lucy's blond hair shone in gleaming contrast to the dark red velvet. Bright red ribbons flowed down the front of the dress, beneath a white lace collar.

"You look lovely," she told Lucy, standing her in front of the mirror so that she could see herself.

"Will the lady like me?" Lucy asked, frowning at her reflection.

"Angela? I'm sure she'll adore you." Sherrie gave the child a hug, then took hold of her hand. "Come on, let's go down and find out what she thinks of you."

Much to Sherrie's satisfaction, and Lucy's shy delight, Angela exclaimed in admiration when she saw the little girl. "Lucy, you look absolutely beautiful," she said, sitting the child on a chair. "You are going to make a wonderful portrait."

The door opened suddenly, making Sherrie jump.

"I'm going to need some help," Matt said, his eyes widening when he saw his daughter. He stared at her for a moment before adding, "I haven't seen that dress before."

"I bought it for her," Sherrie said, as Lucy looked anxious. "Don't you think she looks beautiful?"

"Stunning," Matt agreed. "I hardly recognized you, princess."

Lucy giggled, and Angela said brightly, "She looks adorable. You have excellent taste, Sherrie."

Pleased with herself, Sherrie glanced at Matt. He was looking at her with an odd expression in his eyes.

"I need some help with the tree," he said, giving her no choice but to agree.

"Go ahead," Angela said, as Sherrie hesitated. "Lucy and I will be just fine in here, won't we, honey?"

Lucy nodded, her eyes wide and trusting as she looked upon the artist's face.

"I'll check back in a little while," Sherrie said, feeling as if she were deserting the child. On the other hand, the prospect of helping Matt decorate the tree was too gratifying to miss.

Following him to the living room, Sherrie's skin tingled with the sheer pleasure of looking at him. Even from the back he was impressive. He carried himself so well, with his shoulders pulled back and his dark head held high. She wondered if he'd been in the military, and decided to ask him if she got the chance.

She realized how little she knew about him, considering she was living in the same house with him. She'd taken care to avoid bumping into him in the mornings, and the evenings with Lucy hardly gave them time to talk about anything really personal.

Matt stood back at the living-room door, allowing her to go in first. She felt a shiver of excitement when he closed the door firmly behind him, enclosing them in the quiet intimacy of the room.

The first thing she saw was a magnificent fir standing in one corner. The lights had been turned down low, and the dark green branches gleamed in the glow from the flames in the fireplace. He must have brought in the tree while she was dressing Lucy, Sherrie thought.

The pungent fragrance of fresh pine brought a breath of the outdoors to the cozy room, and Sherrie gasped in delight. "It's beautiful!"

"I'm happy with it," Matt said, sounding pleased. "I didn't want to decorate it by myself. Mrs. Halloway and Lucy usually help me."

"I'll be happy to help you." Sherrie reached for a large box standing in the middle of the floor. "Are the ornaments in here? Shouldn't we wait for Lucy?"

"Of course we'll wait for her. But first I want to put up the lights." Matt dragged a footstool over to the tree. "If you hand them up to me, I'll put them on."

"Good move," Sherrie murmured, lifting out a tangle of wires and lights from the box. "If I got up there I'd probably hang myself with this lot."

"I'm afraid they're in a mess. I just threw them back in the box last year," Matt said, moving toward her. "Here, let me help get them sorted out." He took one end of the tangled mass, while Sherrie found a plug in the other end, and started threading it through the loops.

Her fingers wouldn't seem to cooperate. He'd lowered his head as he concentrated on the twisted wires. He was close enough for her to smell the fragrance of his cologne. His strong fingers worked decisively on the knots, just an inch or so from hers.

She found herself staring at his hands, wondering how they would feel on her bare skin. Her shiver shuddered down her entire body.

Matt raised his head, his electric blue gaze setting off fireworks in her head. "Are you cold?"

"No," she said, her voice barely above a whisper.

She saw the questioning look in his eyes change to one of recognition. She didn't care. It didn't matter anymore if he knew how she felt.

She wanted this man. She wanted to spend the rest of her life with him. She wanted to fall asleep every night snuggled against his back. She wanted to wake up next to him every morning.

She wanted his children, and she wanted Lucy, too. Not only because she loved her, but because she was part of him. It all added up to one inescapable fact. Dammit, she was in love with the man.

Time lost all meaning as she stared into his face. He seemed frozen to the spot, his hands motionless, his uneven breathing barely audible in the quiet stillness of the room.

She lowered her gaze to his mouth, remembering the impact of the brief kiss they'd shared. She wanted to say something, needed to say something, yet could think of nothing.

She longed to lean forward and touch her lips to his, but was afraid of breaking the spell—the flimsy, intangible thread that linked them for those few, precious seconds.

It was Matt who shattered the fragile bond. He blinked, as if trying to clear the fog from his mind. His hands dropped to his sides as he stepped back, leaving her holding the tangled web of lights. "I'll let you finish that while I sort out these ornaments," he said, his voice deliberately casual.

Still shaken by the revelation of her true feelings, she could only nod. He moved away, and started rummaging in the box, bringing out some smaller boxes, which he stacked on the armchair.

She felt cold now, in spite of the warmth of the room. He had warned her, and she hadn't listened. She'd gone barging recklessly into his life, and left herself wide open as usual. Only this time, she faced a far greater heartache than anything Jason could have caused her.

Impatiently she shook the jumbled lights, trying to ease out the knots in them. If only she could rid herself as easily of the knots twisting in her heart.

She hadn't really been in love with Jason, she knew that now. Jason had become a habit that was too hard to break, until he'd dumped her. She had never felt for him the deep, aching need that she felt for Matt.

Why, she wondered fiercely, did she have to find the right man, only to find out that she was the wrong woman? It was the story of her life. She tugged on the lights, and finally, the strings began to loosen up.

Matt was still rummaging in the box, sorting through the ornaments. He looked up as the lights clacked together on the floor. "Got them undone? Good job."

She held them up for his inspection, and he nodded his approval. "Okay, let's get them on the tree before they tangle up again."

"Shouldn't we plug them in first, to see if they work?" she asked, without much enthusiasm. Somehow the thrill had gone out of the task now.

"Good idea. Why didn't I think of that? There's nothing worse than getting the darn things all set up on the tree and then having them not work."

They were talking like strangers again. She watched him climb up on the footstool, the end of the lights in his hand. He had to reach high for the top of the tree. Seeing his lean, strong body stretched to the limit, every contour outlined by the straining fabric of his pants and shirt, she felt such a tug of longing she had to look away.

"I hope you like Lucy's new dress," she said, determined to break the awkward silence that had fallen between them. "I bought it especially for the portrait."

"It's very pretty," he said, glancing down at her from his lofty perch. He reached out and pushed another strand of the lights between the thick branches. "That was a generous thing to do."

"I wanted her to look nice, since she'll be captured for posterity." She was tempted to tell him the portrait was for him, but she wanted more for it to be a surprise.

"I must admit," Matt said, his voice sounding strained as he balanced awkwardly on the stool to reach a distant branch, "your artist friend is a very attractive woman."

Sherrie stifled an unexpected pang of jealousy. "Angela Danvers is not exactly a friend," she said warily. "I just met her for the first time tonight."

"Ah, yes, so you said. You won the portrait, right?"

"Right," she said, feeling uncomfortable with the lie. "Angela was doing a special promotion for her art gallery."

"She has a gallery?"

He sounded really interested, Sherrie thought, trying her best not to be upset by that. She decided it was time to change the subject. "There's one more string," she said, handing it up to him. "I'll get it."

She was halfway across the room when he said quietly, "Then she really isn't one of your matchmaking efforts?"

"No," Sherrie said, pausing to look back at him. "She's not. I didn't even think about that. I'm sorry that I ever thought about it. It was a mistake. I just wanted to give Lucy her wish. I guess I didn't think things through too carefully, as usual."

Matt climbed down and moved toward her. "Don't be so hard on yourself. You meant well."

"I always mean well," Sherrie muttered. She noticed a small box, its clear plastic lid revealing a tiny silver mouse clinging to a gold bell. Engraved on the bell were the words, *For Your Very First Christmas.*

With a murmur of delight she took it out and held it up. "Look at this. Was this for Lucy's first Christmas?"

Matt looked at it, his mouth curving into a smile. He reached out and took it from her, making her shiver as his warm fingers brushed hers.

"Yes, it was," he said softly. "She was ten months old. It was the only Christmas her mother spent with her."

Sherrie felt a stirring of anger at the thought of any woman leaving this man to take care of a helpless baby. "I'm sorry," she whispered.

He shrugged. "It was over a long time ago. Lucy doesn't even remember her."

"I know," Sherrie said unhappily. "That's what's so sad."

Matt looked down at her, and again her pulse leapt at the expression in his eyes. "Sherrie Latimer," he said softly, "you have a heart as big as the universe. It's too bad you haven't met anyone who can appreciate that."

She didn't want anyone else, Sherrie thought miserably. She wanted him. And all he saw when he looked at her was an awkward, irresponsible kid. She was only eleven years younger than him, yet there were times he treated her as if she were a teenager.

Maybe if she were tall and graceful like Angela Danvers, he'd see her in a different light. But then she didn't want to be like Angela Danvers. She wanted him to love her for herself.

Once more her thoughts must have shown in her eyes, as his smile faded. He looked sad, the same kind of look she'd noticed on his face when he watched the kids and their mothers shopping in the toy department.

"You must miss her very much," she said, before she could hold the words back.

He looked down at the ornament in his hands. "No," he said gruffly, "I don't. I never had much of a marriage to begin with. Caroline was too young to take on the responsibilities of a home and family. I should have realized that. I asked too much of her, and she wasn't able to give it. It wasn't entirely her fault."

"Doesn't she ever visit Lucy? I can't understand a mother ever giving up her child."

Matt uttered a dry laugh. "You have to know Caroline to understand. A child would have cramped her style. She gave up custody when I divorced her, and then took off for Europe with a Swiss ski instructor. I never heard from her again."

Sherrie's heart ached for him. "How that must have hurt. But it would have hurt so much more if you had lost Lucy, too. She is a terrific little girl, and she loves you so much. It must be wonderful to have the love of a child."

He looked at her for a long moment, then her heart began to race as he lowered his head and gave her a brief, gentle kiss on the lips. "Merry Christmas, Sherrie," he said softly.

"Merry Christmas, Matt." Her lips trembled so much she could hardly speak the words.

He gave her a long, deep look filled with sadness. His voice was husky, breaking on the words when he spoke. "I'm sorry, Sherrie. I can't—"

The door burst open, shattering the moment. Whatever he was going to say was lost in the flurry of movement as Lucy dashed in, demanding to help with the tree.

She didn't need to ask him what it was he wanted to tell her. She knew what he was going to say. He had realized how she felt about him, and he was trying to tell her that he couldn't return those feelings. She had to accept that and go on with her life without him.

And this time, she knew without a doubt, she wouldn't get over him the way she had Jason. In fact, she doubted if she would ever be quite the same again.

# Chapter Ten

Angela followed Lucy into the room, and stood talking to Matt for a few minutes while Sherrie was helping the little girl sort out the rest of the ornaments. Watching them out of the corner of her eye, Sherrie had to admit that Matt and Angela looked good together.

They were discussing the slow rate of business in the town, and Matt listened intently, his head on one side, his eyes on the artist's lovely face as she explained how her sales were down for the second season in a row.

"Ever since my husband died three years ago," she told Matt, "the business has gone down. I'm afraid if this keeps up I'll have to sell the gallery."

"I'm sure it will turn around again," Matt assured her. "I've seen it happen at the store so many times. We get a couple of bad years and then it picks up again."

"I hope so." Angela uttered a languid sigh. "I don't know what I would do without the gallery."

"I'm sure someone with your talents will find something else," Matt said easily.

Sherrie jumped as Lucy tugged her hand. "Where shall I put this one, Sherrie?"

Aware that she'd been paying far too much attention to Matt's conversation with Angela, Sherrie guided Lucy's hand to an empty branch. "Here, sweetheart, I think this would be the perfect place."

She heard Angela announce that she was leaving, and was about to offer her help when Matt said lightly, "I'll be happy to carry your stuff out for you."

"Oh, would you? That would be such a help." Angela turned a glowing face toward Sherrie. "I'll be back tomorrow night at the same time," she said, and blew Lucy a kiss. "Thank you, Lucy, you behaved beautifully."

Lucy grinned happily at her. "'Night, Angela."

Sherrie watched her leave, with Matt close behind. She heard their voices as they walked up the hallway together, and it was the loneliest sound in the world.

Matt came back into the room a short time later, his face wreathed in smiles. "It's getting cold out there," he said, rubbing his hands together to get them warm.

"Perhaps we'll have snow for Christmas." Sherrie hooked another ornament onto a branch.

Lucy let out a shriek of excitement. "Yay! Then I can slide down the hill on my sled."

"Angela seems to be a nice lady," Matt said, moving closer to the fire. "It's a shame she lost her husband so young."

"Yes, it is." Sherrie swallowed hard. "She must be lonely."

"Especially since she had no children from the marriage."

Fighting her resentment, Sherrie scowled at his back. It sounded as if the two of them had enjoyed a personal conversation out there. She shouldn't mind about that, but she did.

She picked up a package of icicles and ripped it open. Wouldn't it be ironic, she thought viciously, if after all her efforts, Angela Danvers, a woman she'd innocently invited into the house, turned out to be Lucy's new mother.

Mad with herself for caring so much, she flung a handful of tinsel onto the tree. It missed the branch and landed on Lucy's head. Lucy laughed up at her, peering through the silvery strands that hung over her face.

Sherrie's resentment melted. How could she be so selfish, she thought as she hugged the child. It looked as if Lucy might get her wish after all, and if she couldn't be the one, then she couldn't think of anyone better than Angela Danvers.

Looking up, she saw Matt watching her, and the warm expression on his face just about broke her heart. "I think I'd better get Lucy to bed now," she said unsteadily. "It's getting late."

She led the child from the room, wondering how she was going to get through the next two weeks until Christmas Eve, when she would have to say goodbye to the little girl who'd stolen her heart, and the man she loved above all else.

As the days slipped by, Sherrie found it harder and harder to hide her depression. Even Lucy asked her if she was getting sick, while Matt sent her worried glances every now and again when he thought she wasn't looking.

She did her best, but it was hard watching all the excited children and the cheerful shoppers getting ready for the big day. It was hard knowing she would be spending Christmas alone in an empty apartment while everyone else was enjoying the day with their families.

She missed her parents, though they had been gone a good many years. She missed her old friends. She even missed Tom. The only person she didn't miss was Jason, though there were times when she felt a spasm of nostalgia for the good times they'd had. At least she'd been reasonably happy then.

What was hardest of all was watching Matt and Angela together. They seemed to have become good friends in the time they shared talking to each other, and Sherrie's heart ached every time Matt walked the artist to her car.

To make matters worse, every evening after Angela had left, Lucy spent most of her bathtime with Sherrie talking about the fun she had with the artist. It was obvious Lucy adored the woman. It seemed to Sherrie as if she were gradually being shut out of the Blanchards' life, and that hurt.

In spite of her misery, the more she talked to Angela, the more she liked her, and it was impossible to hold any resentment toward the friendly, warmhearted woman.

She could understand Matt's attraction to the artist. He had so much in common with her. They were close to the same age, they shared the same interests and she was an intelligent, charming, attractive woman who obviously enjoyed his company. She was also patient and understanding with Lucy, who quickly became bored with sitting still for such a long time, and had to be coaxed into staying in her chair long enough to get the work done.

Angela would let no one see the portrait until it was finished. Not even Lucy had been allowed to peek, and Sherrie could hardly wait to see the completed painting.

Then, at last, Angela announced that the sittings were over. She would finish the portrait at home, and let her know when it was finished, she told Sherrie.

The call came on the morning of Christmas Eve, just as Sherrie was putting the last of her belongings into her suitcase. Matt had already left for the store, and Lucy was eating her breakfast before leaving for her last day at kindergarten.

"The portrait is finished," Angela said when Sherrie answered the phone. "It's all wrapped, and I can bring it over this evening."

"That's wonderful." Sherrie blinked hard to hold back the tears. She wouldn't be there to see Matt open his gift, but just maybe he'd think of her now and then when he looked at the portrait of his daughter.

"You'll need to write the card," Angela said, "I'm sure you want to do that yourself."

"No," Sherrie said miserably. "I'm not coming back to the house after today. Would you mind writing it for me?"

"Of course. What do you want me to say?"

Sherrie hesitated. There was so much she wanted to say, and none of it was appropriate. "Just say it's from Sherrie, and wish him a Merry Christmas."

"With love?"

Sherrie closed her eyes, finding it impossible to answer.

"You do love him, don't you?" Angela said softly.

Sherrie drew in her breath, then let it out on a trembling sigh. "I have to go now, Angela. I have to take Lucy to kindergarten. Thanks for everything, and…

Merry Christmas.'' She hung up before she broke down completely.

Lucy sat at the kitchen table with her cereal half-eaten. "Are you leaving us?" she asked, her voice trembling on the brink of tears.

Sherrie rushed over to the little girl and put her arms around her. "I'm sorry, sweetheart, but I told you I have another job waiting for me. Mrs. Halloway will be back soon, though, and you'll soon forget all about me."

"I'll never forget you," Lucy said fiercely, tears spilling from her eyes. "Never, never, never."

Those words echoed over and over in Sherrie's head as she sat in Mrs. Claus's chair, doing her best to deal with boisterous, impatient children who were tired of waiting for Christmas.

Now that her last day as Mrs. Claus was coming to an end, she knew she would miss seeing the children and talking to them every day. The bittersweet memories would stay with her forever.

Every year at this time, whenever she saw children lining up to talk to Santa, she would remember Lucy's earnest face wishing for a mom for Christmas. And every year her heart would ache for a very special man.

Then, finally, the moment she had dreaded arrived. From across the crowded floor she saw Matt weaving in and out of the jostling customers, leading Lucy by the hand.

She had been braced for the parting with the little girl all day, and she prayed she would get through it without breaking down. The last thing she wanted to do was upset Lucy any more than she was already.

She almost lost it when she remembered that in a short while she would be saying goodbye to Matt as well. She had to stop by the office to pick up her housekeeping check, and then it would be over. It might as well be her life that was over, she thought as she watched Matt's tall, lean figure striding toward her.

As he came closer, she noticed how tired and strained he looked. It was the first time she'd really looked at him in days, and she wondered what it was that weighed so heavily on his mind.

She wondered if things were not going so well with Angela now that she wasn't at the house every night. She couldn't prevent the little flutter of hope, then was immediately ashamed of herself.

Her feelings were not important in this. It was Lucy who mattered. Lucy and her Christmas wish. It occurred to her then that Lucy hadn't mentioned her wish in some time. Before she could dwell on that, however, Matt had reached her.

"I'll wait for her in the toy department," he said as Lucy climbed up on her lap.

His expression was carefully blank, and Sherrie nodded, trying to hide her heartbreak as she looked down at the little girl. "Well," she said, making her voice determinedly bright, "you look too sad for a little girl on Christmas Eve. Aren't you excited about Santa coming tonight?"

Lucy lifted one of her shoulders in a lopsided shrug. "I guess."

"Well, I know I'm looking forward to going home to the North Pole," Sherrie said cheerfully. "I haven't seen Santa in such a long time, and he's going to be awfully busy tonight, so I guess I won't get to see him until Christmas morning."

"You're not Mrs. Claus," Lucy said in a calm voice.

Sherrie's heart dropped. "Of course I am. Don't let Santa hear you say that, he might—"

"I know who you are." Lucy wore her grave expression as she looked into Sherrie's face. "You're Sherrie."

There wasn't much point in trying to fool the child now, Sherrie thought dismally. All she could hope for was to protect the child's belief in Santa. "When did you guess?" she said, trying to make it sound like a game.

"I dunno." Lucy's lower lip trembled and tears glistened in the corners of her eyes. "I'm gonna miss you, Mrs. Claus. But I'm gonna miss Sherrie even more."

"Oh, honey." Sherrie folded her arms around the little girl and held her close, resting her chin on top of the soft curls. "I'll miss you, too."

Lucy's voice sounded muffled when she answered. "Will you come visit me after Christmas?"

Sherrie closed her eyes as the ache in her heart intensified. That was a promise she couldn't give the little girl. Much as she would love to see her again, she couldn't bear to be around Matt, especially if he was becoming involved with Angela Danvers. It would be too painful.

She gave Lucy the standard answer. "We'll see, sweetheart. That's all I can say right now." She lifted her head and leaned back to look at Lucy's sad little face. "Now I want you to promise me that you'll cheer up. I'm sorry I couldn't find you a mommy in time for Christmas, but I know Santa is going to bring you some wonderful gifts."

Lucy sniffed. "Why did you pr'tend to be Mrs. Claus?"

Sherrie thought quickly. "Well, Santa was too busy to come himself, and Mrs. Claus didn't know how to drive the sleigh, so she asked me if I'd talk to the children for her and let her know what they wanted for Christmas."

Lucy sniffed. "You know the real Mrs. Claus?"

Sherrie forced a smile. "You bet I do." A vision of Angela Danvers, wearing a sparkling rhinestone clasp in her hair, popped into her head. "And I told Mrs. Claus all about your wish. She promised me that she'd try to do something about it real soon, okay?"

Lucy nodded, though a tear spilled from her eye and drifted down her cheek.

"Don't cry, sweetheart." Sherrie leaned down and kissed the tear away. "It's Christmas. Everyone should be happy at Christmas. Especially little girls."

"Daddy's not happy," Lucy said, rubbing her nose with the back of her hand. "He's miser'ble."

Sherrie's heart turned over. So maybe things had gone wrong with Angela after all. She remembered Angela's words on the phone that morning. *You do love him, don't you?* "I'm sorry, honey," she said helplessly. "Perhaps he'll cheer up when he sees what Santa brought him."

She had no chance to say more. She caught sight of Matt standing by the toy shelves, and saw him glance at his watch. "Daddy's waiting for you, sweetheart," she said to Lucy, who appeared to have stopped crying for the moment. "You have a wonderful Christmas, okay? And if you should happen to see Santa tonight, tell him I did the very best job I could for him."

She gave Lucy a final hug, hoping the child hadn't noticed the way her voice had cracked on the last words.

The little girl clung to Sherrie's padding for a long moment before scrambling down to run over to her father. The last Sherrie saw of her, she was clinging to his hand as he led her away to the elevators. She didn't look back.

Sherrie was glad of that. She didn't want Lucy to see Mrs. Claus crying.

At long last, it was time to say goodbye to her job at Blanchard's. Sherrie closed the little gate that led to her chair, then paused to take one last look around her tiny domain. She sent a silent farewell to Donna and Blitzen, the elves peeking out from the windows of the gingerbread house, and the figure of Santa waving goodbye to her from the door.

She took a last, long look at the laden Christmas tree, then patted the red velvet chair. It had been quite an experience, and one she wouldn't have missed for the world.

Slowly she made her way to the elevators, wondering if she'd be able to find Beryl to wish her a Merry Christmas. She had one more ordeal to get through, she told herself, and then she could leave Blanchard's Department Store, never to return.

She would find an apartment on the opposite side of town, and shop in the mall. She need never set foot in Blanchard's Department Store again.

People smiled at her and children grinned shyly at her as the elevator soared upward. Finally left alone to ride to the executive floor, Sherrie thought about the fun it had been to hide behind another guise, while being recognized by so many people. After today she would be back to being Sherrie Latimer, unnoticed by anyone except for the few people who knew her.

Trying desperately to shake off her melancholy, Sherrie headed for the employees' lounge. It was empty, and she changed back into her street clothes, wishing the next few minutes were over. It would be so hard to see Matt again, knowing it would be for the last time.

Lucy would be there, too, which would make it even more difficult to say goodbye. She could only hope that Lucy wouldn't cry.

One thing she wouldn't do, she vowed, was let either of them know how much she was hurting inside. She was going out with her head held high, and her feet on the ground. She'd survived setbacks before and she would survive this one.

For the last time she hung her Mrs. Claus dress on the hanger, and piled the pillows she'd been given for padding on the chair. Carefully she laid out the wig and glasses, and gave them a final pat. "Goodbye, Mrs. Claus," she whispered softly. "It was a pleasure and a privilege to know you."

She took one last long look at herself in the mirror, then, satisfied that she was reasonably presentable, she headed out the door and down the hallway to Matt's office.

Tapping lightly on the door, she stuck her head around and said brightly, "Am I interrupting anything?"

He sat at his desk as usual, punching the keys of his laptop. He looked up as she spoke, and gave her a heartbreaking smile. "Nothing that can't wait. Come on in."

She ventured into the room, her heart sinking when she realized Matt was alone. "Where's Lucy?"

"She's with Beryl," Matt said, closing the lid of his laptop. "She had some last-minute shopping to do."

She would have to try to find her in the store to say goodbye, Sherrie thought, her spirits plummeting even further. She'd hoped to say her goodbyes and get out of there.

"I just stopped in to say goodbye," she said, dismayed at the little catch in her voice. "And to pick up my check, of course."

He nodded, and opened up a file that lay next to his elbow. "Here, it's all made out. Merry Christmas, Mrs.

Claus, and thanks. You'll find your salary for the housekeeping in there, as well as a small bonus.''

She felt chilled. She would have preferred something a little more personal. The bonus made it very clear that she was just an employee to him, and nothing more.

"Well," she said briskly, "I won't keep you. I hope you have a wonderful Christmas and—"

"What are you doing for dinner tomorrow?" Matt asked abruptly.

Caught by surprise, she started stammering. "Well, I haven't...I...er...I guess I'll cook dinner..."

"Well, that's what I wanted to talk to you about." Matt pushed his chair away from the desk and leaned back. "Usually I take Lucy out for Christmas dinner, since Mrs. Halloway always has the time off. But this year I thought it would make a nice change to have dinner at home. It's more relaxing, don't you think?"

Sherrie nodded warily, wondering what was coming.

"So," Matt said, getting to his feet, "I wondered if you'd come over and cook Christmas dinner for us."

She stared at him, unable to believe what she'd heard. For the life of her she couldn't think of a word to say.

"I know it's short notice," Matt said, "but as long as you're not doing anything else..."

His voice trailed off as Sherrie slowly lifted her chin. She'd had all she could take from Matthew Blanchard and his damned indifference to her feelings. She was no longer his employee, and she had nothing to lose. She was tired of being taken for granted.

Bracing her shoulders, she pulled in a deep breath. "I don't know what gives you the impression that I have nothing better to do tomorrow than cook dinner for you. As a matter of fact, I do have other plans. Why don't you ask Angela to cook dinner for you? I'm sure she would love to spend the day with you."

Matt blinked. "Angela?"

She hadn't meant to say that. It had just slipped out. Furious with herself, she said lamely, "Well, I just thought, since you and she—"

She broke off at Matt's incredulous look. "You think I'm interested in Angela?"

He moved around the edge of the desk, and she backed up a step or two. She was floundering badly, and she knew it. "I only meant that since she's on her own, and you're on your own, and you seem to...well...you know."

"No," Matt said grimly, "I don't know. Why don't you tell me?"

He moved closer, and again she stepped back. "I just thought she might enjoy spending the day with you and Lucy," she said weakly.

"Really." He kept moving forward and she kept stepping back, until finally she came up against the door.

"Well," she said a little desperately, "I guess you'll have to go out for dinner, after all."

"Perhaps. But I rather doubt it."

Her heart started pounding as Matt kept coming until he was standing almost toe-to-toe with her. His eyes looked as blue as a warm, tropical sea, and she saw a gleam of determination in his gaze that threatened to stop her heartbeat.

She was not going to let him kiss her again, she told herself fiercely. She was not going to kiss him again. She'd been hurt enough, and Christmas or not, she was not going to let him indulge in a lighthearted kiss simply in the spirit of the season.

"I don't want Angela to spend Christmas Day with me," Matt said softly. "I want you to spend the day with me."

Helplessly she watched his mouth as he moved in to take her in his arms. She wanted nothing more in the world than to feel that mouth on hers. Even so, a small vestige of her pride still remained. "I told you," she said breathlessly, "I have better things to do."

"Better than this?" Matt murmured, and lowered his mouth to hers. His kiss was feather-soft, brushing her lips in a tantalizing promise of more to come.

She made a feeble effort to pull back, but his arms held her fast against his chest. "I don't think we should be doing this," she said, her pulse flying when she saw the smile hovering around his incredible mouth. "What if Lucy comes in?"

"Lucy won't come in." He lowered his voice to a husky murmur that took the strength from her knees. "I made sure of that."

"Oh." She sent a desperate glance over his shoulder at the clock. "Well, I really should be going—"

"Not until I tell you what I've been waiting to tell you all day." Again his mouth descended on hers, and this time there was nothing gentle about it.

She felt all the resistance draining out of her body as he wrapped his arms closer around her and kissed her with all the pent-up hunger of a man who has waited too long.

Stars seemed to dance around her head as she finally gave up the struggle and met his passion with an eagerness of her own. She saw snowflakes and moonbeams, heard angels singing and bells ringing, and felt the warmth of love and the fire of need.

His arms tightened around her, his mouth grew more demanding and she was sure she would never breathe properly again. She wanted to go on kissing him forever, and never come back to earth. For somewhere in the back of her mind, she knew that pain was waiting for her when she did return.

He finally lifted his head, though his arms still held her tight as he gazed down at her.

Her heart soared, then hovered uncertainly as she watched his face. If only she could believe the desire she saw in his eyes, the passion heating his face.

"I should have done that a long time ago," he said thickly. "Maybe then, you wouldn't have been so hell-bent on getting me married off to someone else."

"Why didn't you?" she said, trying her best to breathe properly.

His lips twitched, as if he were hiding a grin. "I make it a point never to make a move on one of my employees."

"Oh." She thought about that for a moment. "Is that the only reason?"

He sighed and dropped another brief kiss on her lips before letting her go. "No, it's not the only reason." He moved back to his desk and sank his hips down on the edge of it. "I guess I was afraid of making another mistake."

Her heart began to pound as she stared at him. What was he trying to tell her? Afraid to hope, afraid to believe, her lips barely moved as she whispered, "So am I."

Her heart stopped beating altogether as he lifted his arms and held them out to her. "Come here," he said softly.

She took a step closer to him. "Matt, I...hope you're not doing all this just to get me to cook dinner for you."

It was a stupid thing to say, and not what she meant to say at all.

His eyebrows shot up, and he lowered his arms. Slowly, he eased himself up from the desk. "I guess I deserve that," he said quietly.

"I'm sorry." She felt the tears trembling on her lids and blinked them away. "I just—"

"Sherrie." He moved quickly, closing the distance between them as he reached for her. "I'm not making myself clear. Yes, I am doing this so that you'll cook dinner for Lucy and me tomorrow."

She stiffened, but he held her tight, refusing to let her pull away. "I want you to cook dinner for us tomorrow, and the day after that—" he feathered her lips with his "—and the day after that—" again he set her on fire with his kiss "—and the day after that, until the end of time."

She whimpered, then threw her arms around his neck and clung to him, tears of joy spilling down her cheeks as she kissed him back.

When he could breathe again, he held her head against his chest and said huskily, "I finally realized what I should have admitted all along, when you were parading those women up and down in front of me. I wasn't interested in any of them because my heart had been stolen by a miniature Santa in ridiculous high-heeled shoes."

"You were so mad at me that day," Sherrie said, mumbling against his chest. "You were mad at me a lot."

"Mad about you, more like it," Matt said wryly. "You were driving me crazy, but not in the way you think. I wanted you from the moment I first saw you without your Santa wig."

She drew back to look up at him, her body trembling with the wild excitement of being in his arms. "You had a very strange way of showing it," she said.

"I did my damnedest to ignore it," Matt said. "I might have known it was a losing battle." His face grew serious, and the look in his eyes chased away the last of her doubts.

"You wanted to make Lucy's Christmas wish come true. I have a Christmas wish, too. You'd make Lucy and me very happy if you'd make them both come true. Lucy needs a mom, and I need a wife. Would you be willing to take us both on?"

Now she was crying in earnest, but it didn't matter any more. They were tears of happiness—of sheer, unbelievable joy. Winding her arms around his neck again, she said tearfully, "I thought you'd never ask."

Matt's eyes looked suspiciously damp, too, as he looked down at her. "Does that mean you will marry us?"

"If you don't mind marrying a klutz."

"The most adorable, warmhearted, lovable klutz I've ever met."

"How many have you—" Sherrie began, but his kiss prevented her from finishing the question. It was some time later before she remembered Lucy.

"When are you going to tell her?" she asked, wondering what the little girl would say when she heard the news.

"We're going to tell her as soon as she gets back." Matt pulled her over to his chair and sat her down in it. "She's going to be a little surprised, I think, but very, very happy. Just like me." He sat on the arm of the chair and dropped a kiss on her forehead.

"I think she's really fond of Angela," Sherrie said, reaching for his hand.

He clasped his fingers around hers and squeezed. 'Angela has become a very good friend. It was Angela who made me realize how much you meant to me."

Sherrie looked up in surprise. "She did?"

Matt smiled, and lifted her fingers to his mouth to kiss them. "The closer it got to Christmas Eve, the more miserable I felt. I wouldn't admit to myself that it was because you would be leaving, and I probably wouldn't see you again."

He leaned his head back and let out a long sigh. "I kept telling myself that it was for the best, and that once the Christmas season was over I could forget you, but deep down I knew I was fooling myself. Even then, I fought it."

She looked up at him, still finding it hard to believe he'd actually asked her to marry him. "How did Angela know how you felt?"

"She knew I was miserable, and guessed the reason. She told me I had better do something about it, before it was too late. She hinted that you would be happy about that."

Sherrie nodded. "She knew I was in love with you. I guess it was obvious to everyone except ourselves. Even Maria guessed how I felt about you."

"I think we were both doing our best to deny it. I kept telling myself that I didn't want Lucy hurt again, but I know that was just a cop-out. I was the one afraid of getting hurt again."

Sherrie sighed. "What a lot of time we wasted."

"Well, let's not waste any more. How about a Valentine's wedding?"

She'd thought that she couldn't be any happier. She'd been wrong. "I think that sounds perfect," she said unsteadily.

He peered down at her. "You're sure? You're taking on a ready-made family, you know."

"I'm sure." She peeked up at him. "What about you? I just hope you're not doing all this just to get a permanent housekeeper."

This time he smiled. "As a matter of fact, I thought we'd keep on Mrs. Halloway. I thought you might like to keep your job at Conway Pharmaceuticals."

Sherrie's heart lifted with joy. "I'd like to keep working," she said, "but only until we can give Lucy a baby brother or sister, or two."

"Or three?" Matt murmured, and lowered his head once more, leaving her in no doubt that this time her plan met with his complete approval.

Tomorrow, she thought happily as she melted in his arms, was going to be the most wonderful Christmas of all.

# *Epilogue*

They didn't tell Lucy that afternoon, after all. Sherrie had a much better idea. It was hard not to let the little girl see the happiness blazing in her heart, but Sherrie managed to sound convincing when she explained to Lucy that she was staying just long enough to cook Christmas dinner the next day.

"You must close your eyes now," she told the little girl at bedtime that evening. "Santa won't come unless you're asleep."

"I don't care," Lucy said, jutting out her lower lip. "It's going to be a miser'ble Christmas, anyway."

Tucking the covers close around the little body, Sherrie bent down and kissed Lucy's forehead. "Remember that miracles happen at Christmastime," she whispered. "Maybe Santa will bring you your wish."

Lucy looked gravely up at her. "I don't think Santa knows 'bout my wish," she murmured sleepily.

Sherrie smiled, blew a last kiss and left her to wait for her daddy to say good-night to her.

While Matt was still upstairs with Lucy, Angela arrived with the portrait. Sherrie placed it at the back of the tree, then invited Angela to stay for a glass of sherry.

"I'm visiting some friends tonight," Angela said, "and I'm late now." She looked closer at Sherrie. "Has something happened? You look positively radiant."

Quickly, Sherrie explained.

"I couldn't be more delighted," Angela said, giving her a warm hug. "I just knew that you two were meant for each other."

"I have you to thank." Sherrie's eyes misted as she smiled at her friend. "Matt told me that you suggested he tell me how he felt."

Angela shook her head in mock disgust. "Isn't it incredible how obtuse some men can be?"

"Some women, too," Sherrie said ruefully. "I thought he was interested in you."

Angela's incredulous laugh made her feel better. Until then she hadn't been sure how the attractive artist felt about Matt.

"I'll let you in on a secret," Angela whispered. "I'm meeting my special someone tonight, and I'm hoping he'll pop the question, too. I'll let you know if he does."

Sherrie threw her arms around her friend. "That's fabulous, Angela. I'll keep my fingers crossed."

Angela laughed. "So will I. Now I'd better get going." She headed for the door saying, "Wish Matt and Lucy a very Merry Christmas for me, and you might want to rewrite the card on the portrait now that things have changed for you."

"I will," Sherrie promised. She closed the door behind Angela, then flew back to the living room to change

the card. She barely had time to fasten the new one to th
package before Matt returned.

"Did I hear Angela down here?" he asked, lookin
around the room as if expecting to see her.

"You did, and she left. She had an important engage
ment." Sherrie went happily into his arms and laid he
head against his shoulder. "It's going to be a wonderfu
Christmas for all of us," she murmured.

Lucy awoke early the next morning. Sherrie heard th
stairs creak as the little girl crept down them. Flingin
herself joyfully out of bed, Sherrie threw on her robe an
pounded on Matt's door as she flew past. "Get up, l
zybones," she yelled, "It's Christmas!"

Lucy was standing in the middle of the living roon
staring with wide eyes at the gifts her father and Sherr
had stacked under the tree late the night before. "A doll
house!" she exclaimed in a voice filled with wonde
"I've always wanted a doll's house."

Matt came in just as Lucy discovered the toy horse c
wheels. His smile was casual enough as he greeted the
both, but his eyes skimmed over Sherrie with an appr
ciative gleam in them that warmed her cheeks.

Leaving Lucy to examine the rest of her gifts, Sherr
dragged out the portrait and handed it over to Matt. "
had Angela paint this especially for you," she said, as l
slowly unwrapped it. "I wanted to give you a very sp
cial gift."

"You've already given me the greatest gift I could ev
want," he said softly. "But this is beautiful. Thank yo
darling."

She sent a swift glance at Lucy. "Do you think it
time?"

"I definitely think it's time. I want to kiss you."

Sherrie moved over to the tree and picked up a heart-shaped box from under its branches. "Here, honey," she said, kneeling beside the little girl, "here's one you missed."

Lucy barely glanced at the box. "What is it?"

"I think it's a special gift from Santa," Sherrie said, handing it to her.

Lucy looked up, her eyes brimming with tears. "He didn't bring my special wish," she said, her lip trembling.

"Why don't you open the box, sweetheart," Sherrie said, feeling like crying too.

Lucy struggled with the catch for a moment then lifted the lid. "It's a letter," she said, her voice rising in surprise. "Is it from Santa?"

Matt came forward and took the folded sheet of paper from his daughter. "Well, let's see," he said, frowning at the note. "I guess it *is* from Santa. Would you like me to read it for you?"

Lucy nodded, her gaze fixed earnestly on his face.

Sherrie felt a little squiggle of excitement as he cleared his throat and began to read. "Dear Lucy, Mrs. Claus told me about your very special wish for Christmas, and since you've been a very good girl this year, I've brought you your gift. Her name is Sherrie and she's kneeling there right beside you. She is going to be your very own Christmas mommy."

Lucy's eyes grew wide, and her mouth opened, but no sound came out.

"I hope that's all right with you, sweetheart?" Sherrie asked anxiously.

Lucy's high-pitched squeal almost deafened Sherrie as the little girl threw herself off the horse and fell into her arms. "I wished and *wished* that you'd be my mommy," she said tearfully as her arms closed around Sherrie's neck.

Sherrie couldn't speak. She could only hug the child while tears of joy spilled down her cheeks.

Matt cleared his throat. "I guess it's unanimous," he said huskily.

Sherrie gazed up at his smiling face. "There will never be a more perfect Christmas," she whispered.

\* \* \* \* \*

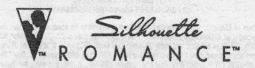

# COMING NEXT MONTH

**#1198 MAD FOR THE DAD—Terry Essig**
*Fabulous Fathers*
He knew next to nothing about raising his infant nephew. So
ingle "dad" Daniel Van Scott asked his lovely new neighbor
Rachel Gatlin for a little advice—and found himself noticing her
charms as both a mother...*and* as a woman.

**#1199 HAVING GABRIEL'S BABY—Kristin Morgan**
*Bundles of Joy*
One fleeting night of passion and Joelle was in the family way!
And now the father of her baby, hardened rancher Gabriel Lafleur,
insisted they marry immediately. But could they find true love
before their bundle of joy arrived?

**#1200 NEW YEAR'S WIFE—Linda Varner**
*Home for the Holidays*
Years ago, the man Julie McCrae had loved declared her too
young for him and walked out of her life. Now Tyler Jordan was
back, and Julie was all woman. But did she dare hope that Tyler
would renew the love they'd once shared, and make her his New
Year's Wife?

**#1201 FAMILY ADDITION—Rebecca Daniels**
Single dad Colt Wyatt thought his little girl, Jenny, was all he
needed in his life, until he met Cassandra Sullivan—the lovely
woman who enchanted his daughter and warmed his heart. But
after so long, would he truly learn to love again and make
Cassandra an addition to his family?

**#1202 ABOUT THAT KISS—Jayne Addison**
Maid of honor Joy Mackey was convinced that Nick Tremain was
out to ruin her sister's wedding. And she was determined to go to
any lengths to see her sis happily wed—even if it meant keeping
Nick busy by marrying him herself!

**#1203 GROOM ON THE LOOSE—Christine Scott**
To save him from scandal, Cassie Andrews agreed to pose as
Greg Lawton's *pretend* significant other. The handsome doctor
was surely too arrogant—and way too sexy—to be real husband
material! Or was this groom just waiting to be tamed?

## FAST CASH 4031 DRAW RULES
### NO PURCHASE OR OBLIGATION NECESSARY

Fifty prizes of $50 each will be awarded in random drawings to be conducted no later than 3/28/97 from amongst all eligible responses to this prize offer received as of 2/14/97. To enter, follow directions, affix 1st-class postage and mail OR write Fast Cash 4031 on a 3" x 5" card along with your name and address and mail that card to: Harlequin's Fast Cash 4031 Draw, P.O. Box 1395, Buffalo, NY 14240-1395 OR P.O. Box 618, Fort Erie, Ontario L2A 5X3. (Limit: one entry per outer envelope; all entries must be sent via 1st-class mail.) Limit: one prize per household. Odds of winning are determined by the number of eligible responses received. Offer is open only to residents of the U.S. (except Puerto Rico) and Canada and is void wherever prohibited by law. All applicable laws and regulations apply. Any litigation within the province of Quebec respecting the conduct and awarding of a prize in this sweepstakes maybe submitted to the Régie des alcools, des courses et des jeux. In order for a Canadian resident to win a prize, that person will be required to correctly answer a time-limited arithmetical skill-testing question to be administered by mail. Names of winners available after 4/28/97 by sending a self-addressed, stamped envelope to: Fast Cash 4031 Draw Winners, P.O. Box 4200, Blair, NE 68009-4200.

## OFFICIAL RULES
## MILLION DOLLAR SWEEPSTAKES
### NO PURCHASE NECESSARY TO ENTER

1. To enter, follow the directions published. Method of entry may vary. For eligibility, entries must be received no later than March 31, 1998. No liability is assumed for printing errors, lost, late, non-delivered or misdirected entries.
   To determine winners, the sweepstakes numbers assigned to submitted entries will be compared against a list of randomly pre-selected prize winning numbers. In the event all prizes are not claimed via the return of prize winning numbers, random drawings will be held from among all other entries received to award unclaimed prizes.

2. Prize winners will be determined no later than June 30, 1998. Selection of winning numbers and random drawings are under the supervision of D. L. Blair, Inc., an independent judging organization whose decisions are final. Limit: one prize to a family or organization. No substitution will be made for any prize, except as offered. Taxes and duties on all prizes are the sole responsibility of winners. Winners will be notified by mail. Odds of winning are determined by the number of eligible entries distributed and received.

3. Sweepstakes open to residents of the U.S. (except Puerto Rico), Canada and Europe who are 18 years of age or older, except employees and immediate family members of Torstar Corp., D. L. Blair, Inc., their affiliates, subsidiaries, and all other agencies, entities, and persons connected with the use, marketing or conduct of this sweepstakes. All applicable laws and regulations apply. Sweepstakes offer void wherever prohibited by law. Any litigation within the province of Quebec respecting the conduct and awarding of a prize in this sweepstakes must be submitted to the Régie des alcools, des courses et des jeux. In order to win a prize, residents of Canada will be required to correctly answer a time-limited arithmetical skill-testing question to be administered by mail.

4. Winners of major prizes (Grand through Fourth) will be obligated to sign and return an Affidavit of Eligibility and Release of Liability within 30 days of notification. In the event of non-compliance within this time period or if a prize is returned as undeliverable, D. L. Blair, Inc. may at its sole discretion award that prize to an alternate winner. By acceptance of their prize, winners consent to use of their names, photographs or other likeness for purposes of advertising, trade and promotion on behalf of Torstar Corp., its affiliates and subsidiaries without further compensation unless prohibited by law. Torstar Corp. and D. L. Blair, Inc. their affiliates and subsidiaries are not responsible for errors in printing of sweepstakes and prizewinning numbers. In the event a duplication of a prizewinning number occurs, a random drawing will be held from among all entries received with that prizewinning number to award that prize.

SWP-S12ZD

5. This sweepstakes is presented by Torstar Corp., its subsidiaries and affiliates in conjunction with book, merchandise and/or product offerings. The number of prizes to be awarded and their value are as follows: Grand Prize — $1,000,000 (payable at $33,333.33 a year for 30 years); First Prize — $50,000; Second Prize — $10,000; Third Prize — $5,000; 3 Fourth Prizes — $1,000 each; 10 Fifth Prizes — $250 each; 1,000 Sixth Prizes — $10 each. Values of all prizes are in U.S. currency. Prizes in each level will be presented in different creative executions, including various currencies, vehicles, merchandise and travel. Any presentation of a prize level in a currency other than U.S. currency represents an approximate equivalent to the U.S. currency prize for that level, at that time. Prize winners will have the opportunity of selecting any prize offered for that level; however, the actual non U.S. currency equivalent prize, if offered and selected, shall be awarded at the exchange rate existing at 3:00 P.M. New York time on March 31, 1998. A travel prize option, if offered and selected by winner, must be completed within 12 months of selection and is subject to: traveling companion(s) completing and returning a Release of Liability prior to travel; and hotel and flight accommodations availability. For a current list of all prize options offered within prize levels, send a self-addressed, stamped envelope (WA residents need not affix postage) to: MILLION DOLLAR SWEEPSTAKES Prize Options, P.O. Box 4456, Blair, NE 68009-4456, USA.

6. For a list of prize winners (available after July 31, 1998) send a separate, stamped, self-addressed envelope to: MILLION DOLLAR SWEEPSTAKES Winners, P.O. Box 4459, Blair, NE 68009-4459, USA.

## EXTRA BONUS PRIZE DRAWING
### NO PURCHASE OR OBLIGATION NECESSARY TO ENTER

7. The Extra Bonus Prize will be awarded in a random drawing to be conducted no later than 5/30/98 from among all entries received. To qualify, entries must be received by 3/31/98 and comply with published directions. Prize ($50,000) is valued in U.S. currency. Prize will be presented in different creative expressions, including various currencies, vehicles, merchandise and travel. Any presentation in a currency other than U.S. currency represents an approximate equivalent to the U.S. currency value at that time. Prize winner will have the opportunity of selecting any prize offered in any presentation of the Extra Bonus Prize Drawing; however, the actual non U.S. currency equivalent prize, if offered and selected by winner, shall be awarded at the exchange rate existing at 3:00 P.M. New York time on March 31, 1998. For a current list of prize options offered, send a self-addressed, stamped envelope (WA residents need not affix postage) to: Extra Bonus Prize Options, P.O. Box 4462, Blair, NE 68009-4462, USA. All eligibility requirements and restrictions of the MILLION DOLLAR SWEEPSTAKES apply. Odds of winning are dependent upon number of eligible entries received. No substitution for prize except as offered. For the name of winner (available after 7/31/98), send a self-addressed, stamped envelope to: Extra Bonus Prize Winner, P.O. Box 4463, Blair, NE 68009-4463, USA.

SWP-S12ZD2

# As seen on TV!
## *Free Gift Offer*

With a Free Gift proof-of-purchase from any Silhouette® book,
you can receive a beautiful cubic zirconia pendant.

This gorgeous marquise-shaped stone is a genuine cubic
zirconia—accented by an 18" gold tone necklace.
(Approximate retail value $19.95)

# Send for yours today...
## compliments of ▼ *Silhouette®*

To receive your free gift, a cubic zirconia pendant, send us one original proof-of-
purchase, photocopies not accepted, from the back of any Silhouette Romance™,
Silhouette Desire®, Silhouette Special Edition®, Silhouette Intimate Moments®
or Silhouette Yours Truly™ title available in August, September, October, November and
December at your favorite retail outlet, together with the Free Gift Certificate, plus a
check or money order for $1.65 U.S./$2.15 CAN. (do not send cash) to cover postage and
handling, payable to Silhouette Free Gift Offer. We will send you the specified gift. Allow
6 to 8 weeks for delivery. Offer good until December 31, 1996 or while quantities last.
Offer valid in the U.S. and Canada only.

## *Free Gift Certificate*

Name: _____

Address: _____

City: _____ State/Province: _____ Zip/Postal Code: _____

Mail this certificate, one proof-of-purchase and a check or money order for postage
and handling to: SILHOUETTE FREE GIFT OFFER 1996. In the U.S.: 3010 Walden
Avenue, P.O. Box 9077, Buffalo NY 14269-9077. In Canada: P.O. Box 613, Fort Erie,
Ontario L2Z 5X3.

---

## FREE GIFT OFFER
084-KMD

ONE PROOF-OF-PURCHASE

To collect your fabulous FREE GIFT, a cubic zirconia pendant, you must include this
original proof-of-purchase for each gift with the properly completed Free Gift Certificate.

084-KMD-R

# You're About to Become a *Privileged Woman*

Reap the rewards of fabulous free gifts and benefits with proofs-of-purchase from Silhouette and Harlequin books

# Pages & Privileges™

It's our way of thanking you for buying our books at your favorite retail stores.

**PROOF OF PURCHASE**
SR-PP20
Offer expires March 31, 1997

### Harlequin and Silhouette— the most privileged readers in the world!

For more information about Harlequin and Silhouette's PAGES & PRIVILEGES program call the Pages & Privileges Benefits Desk: 1-503-794-2499

*Silhouette*®

SR-PP20